THE STRANGER

KIERSTEN MODGLIN

KIERSTEN
MODGLIN

Cover Design by Kiersten Modglin
Copy Editing by Three Owls Editing
Proofreading by My Brother's Editor
Formatting by Kiersten Modglin

First Print and Electronic Edition: 2024
kierstenmodglinauthor.com

To the strangers who've become friends.

"The best way to find out if you can trust somebody is to trust them."

-ERNEST HEMINGWAY

CHAPTER ONE

TIBBY

You've got to be fucking kidding me.

The car in front of me crawls to a slow stop, large snowflakes clinging to every inch of its body. Even in the dark, I can see that it's red. Obnoxious, look-at-me, I-probably-rev-my-engine-at-stop-lights *red*. Its wipers sling back and forth at full speed, doing little to clear the blanket of thick, white snow that seems insistent upon forming on the dark glass. As I pass the car, continuing on my way, I try to stare through the small space on the windshield that's being kept clear to see who's inside, but it's impossible. Everything inside the vehicle is completely dark.

My feet are frozen inside my boots—so cold I can't feel them anymore—and the wet snow has begun to soak through my clothes. I should've dressed more warmly, but I wasn't exactly counting on being out here this long. This entire evening has been one surprise after the next.

My teeth chatter painfully as I stare at the car over my shoulder, refusing to stop moving, though my entire body is aching from the cold, every inch of my exposed skin burning while even what's bundled up aches with something deep in my bones.

Even still, as the car speeds up a little so he's next to me again, and I get a better look at him through the window on the passenger side, I know without a doubt that I'd rather wait several more hours in this ridiculous weather than get in the car with him.

With *any* him, really. It's not that this man is particularly offensive, I suppose. It's just that he's a man in the first place. I may not be the smartest or most intuitive person in a given room, but I know enough to know women are rarely safe in rooms alone with men. Or cars, in this case.

He rolls down the window, keeping pace with me as he leans over in his seat. Blond hair. A little more than a five o'clock shadow across his chin. Charming smile.

It's even worse than I thought.

I wish he had acne and a missing eye. Scars covering ninety percent of his body. A hairy mole. Something, anything, that might warn me of the danger he surely poses to me.

"You need some help?" he shouts over the noise of the wipers and the storm. His voice is warm and masculine but nice. Soft, despite yelling.

I want to trust him, yet I know I can't. My body is at

war with itself as I glance at him one more time. Never again will I be fooled by a handsome smile and kind eyes.

"I'm fine," I shout back, squeezing my hands into fists. *Move the hell along, pal. Nothing to see here.*

He stares at me a while longer, clearly expecting me to say something else, then looks forward through the windshield and back at me. "Are you sure? Do you need a ride somewhere? This storm is brutal."

"It's okay. Thanks, though." I focus on walking before I trip and fall on my face. I've had several close calls already tonight, and I know if I fall and get my clothing wet, I'll freeze to death before I get someplace to warm up. Not that I have any idea where that someplace will be. Already, I'm worried about frostbite on my toes. I wish I'd paid more attention when we read *Call of the Wild* in school; maybe I'd remember more about what frostbite feels like to know when to start panicking.

My boots aren't meant for this as they slosh through the browning snow on the side of the road. They're fake leather, too thin, and it's too cold for them to keep my feet even remotely warm. And even if they do, they'll be ruined by the end of this, if I survive it at all.

To my chagrin, the car continues to ease forward, remaining at my side, and then he's shouting again. "Come on. I can't leave you out here in good conscience. Let me drop you off somewhere. What are you doing out here anyway? Did your car break down?"

"Something like that," I mutter, though my voice is

too low for him to have heard me. I turn my head again, shouting my response. "Seriously, I'm fine."

"You can't be fine. Where could you possibly be walking to? It's too cold for anyone to enjoy this, and I'm sorry, but you aren't dressed nearly warm enough to be out here," he scoffs, but I refuse to look down at the jeans, sweater, and jacket I'm wearing. "At least let me take you somewhere to get gloves and a hat. Maybe I have some in the car with me. Will you just wait a second?"

I do stop then, but not for the reason he thinks. I take a step closer to the car, hands steady at my sides. "Look, you've done your good deed. You stopped, you checked. I'm telling you I'm fine. I don't need your help."

"Where are you going?" he asks, his head tilted toward his shoulder. "Will you at least tell me that? Or... or tell me someone's on their way to pick you up?"

"Fine. Someone's on their way to pick me up," I rattle off.

"Who?"

"My aunt." The lie comes easily.

"What's her name?"

I hesitate, caught off guard. "Sh-Sharon." That lie comes less easily. The pause only lasts a second, but it's enough for him to sense I'm being dishonest.

He runs a hand over his face. "Okay. Look, I'm not sure what is going on here, but the nearest town is still over an hour's drive from where we are. You can't walk.

You won't make it. You'll freeze to death out here and I couldn't live with myself if that happened."

I take another step toward the car, and he must assume he's won, that I'm giving in, because suddenly a small grin fills his lips.

I ruin that good mood quickly, releasing a groan meant to keep myself calm. "I don't know what you aren't understanding, dude. I don't *need* your help. I don't *want* your help. Go." I wave a hand in the air, shooing him away. "Go away. This isn't going to go the way you think it is. You've offered, but I said no. If I don't make it or if something bad happens, that's on me. Your conscience should be clear. You did all you could. Bye now."

He stares ahead, the smile disappearing, and for a moment, I think he's going to leave. Instead, he says, "But why? Why won't you let me help you? I don't know why you're walking this empty highway in the middle of the night, but I know I haven't passed a car on this stretch of road in hours. How long's it been since you saw another car? If you don't trust me, fine, but how long until someone you *do* trust comes along? I swear I'm not trying to hurt you. I just... I can't leave you out here. I'm sorry, but I can't."

I stare at him in utter disbelief. This man really is impossible. Why are we still arguing over this? "What you can or can't do is not my problem. I'm not getting in the car with a stranger. I'll be fine."

He stops the car, his headlights suddenly flashing

bright as he turns on his hazard lights. Then, he steps from the car and jogs over to me, his hand held out. "Hi. I haven't properly introduced myself. I'm Walker."

I force a sickly-sweet smile. "Hi, Walk*er*. I'm walk*ing*." My voice goes flat and emotionless, and I watch as his grin goes away. "And I didn't ask for your help." I ignore his hand and zip around him, continuing to walk and hoping he gets the hint.

He's persistent, I'll give him that. Then again, so are most serial killers.

"Now we aren't strangers," he says. "Though I suspect, and kind of hope, your name isn't literally *walking*."

"Caught onto that, did you?" I shake my head. This is ridiculous. At least he hasn't raced to catch up with me yet.

"You know, if I wanted to hurt you, I wouldn't ask you to get in the car. I'd just take you," he calls from behind me. His words stun me, and I stop in my tracks. Slowly, angrily, I turn around to face him. My nails dig into my palms as I squeeze my hands into fists inside the sleeves of my jacket.

In fairness, he has a point. If he meant me harm, he could easily try to pick me up and shove me into his car. He underestimates my will to survive, however, and the fact that I would fight with everything I have. He thinks I'm just a woman—a helpless, defenseless woman.

Sometimes, I think that's our best weapon. Let them think we're weak until we have to prove otherwise.

"I don't have any weapons on me. Feel free to search my car. I'm not a threat to you. I just want to be sure you're safe. I'd offer to call you a ride, but there's no service out here for miles." He gives a half-shrug as if to say he's thought of everything. "I get that you don't want my help—don't *need* my help—but can you just...can you just get in the car and let me drive you to the nearest town so you can get someone's help?" He laughs through a pleading face. "You're shivering, and it's killing me."

I hadn't realized I was, but now I notice he's right. My body is so cold I've begun to lose feeling everywhere. Freezing isn't a bad way to go, from what I've heard. Just like falling asleep.

For the record, it's not like that's why I'm out here. But it beats being skinned alive or whatever this monster might have in store for me. I'm not an idiot, and his little act of pretending to care doesn't fool me.

"Can you at least tell me your name?"

"Why?" I challenge.

"Hell if I know," he says with a sigh. "But I have this feeling in my gut that if something happens to you, I'll never forgive myself. And, since I'm a southern gentleman, neither will my momma." One corner of his mouth upturns with a charming smile that has worked wonders for him in the past, I'd be willing to bet. "My parents taught me manners, Walking."

At that, I snort. "But obviously not to know that no means no."

His jaw drops open, his finger up in the air. "Now

look, this is not that. I know that no means no. I'm just...
I'm trying to help you. I'm trying to make sure you don't
freeze." I begin to walk again, and this time, he jogs to
catch up. "Unless that's your plan."

I set my jaw, pinning my chin forward. "I'm not
going to freeze."

"Respectfully disagree."

Crossing my arms, I give a sharp nod without
looking at him. "And that's your right."

He scoffs. "Are you really so stubborn you'd let yourself die out here just to avoid getting in the car with me?"

"Better so stubborn than so stupid I get in the car
with a stranger and end up dead."

"Do I really look dangerous to you?" He shoves both
hands out to his sides dramatically.

I cut a quick glance his way without really looking at
him. "You're a white male in your thirties, so if you've
watched the news, like, literally ever, I'm not really sure I
need to answer that question."

He laughs then. I mean really, *really* laughs. His head
falls backward, mouth gaped open as he releases the
warm sound into the night. When he's done, he's winded
and out of breath, like this is a comedy show, and I've just
made his night. As he finally pulls himself together, I
can't believe I'm still standing here. I'm utterly shocked
at how dumb we both are.

"I guess that's a fair point," he says eventually. Then,
as if it's on his side, the storm picks up, icy pellets of
snow smacking me in the face and arms, clinging to my

hair. The wind howls in sync with the voice inside of me screaming that I'm going to freeze to death if I don't find somewhere warm and dry soon.

I'm very concerned about my toes, which no longer have any feeling left. Each step is accompanied by a sharp, lightning sensation in my legs.

I want to survive this. Deep underneath everything else, the fear, the anger, the confusion, I know that I want to make it through this night alive. The question is, how do I do that? What am I supposed to do when I have two paths laid out in front of me, and neither seems safe, though they're my only options.

I could get into the car with him, see what happens, and hope for the best. Or I could keep walking and hope I don't freeze to death. Either way feels awful, but only one of those options seems to have a slight bit of hope to it. Only one of the scenarios seems like at least a fifty percent chance of survival.

He clears his throat, and I realize I've been standing here silently for a very long time. So long that there are now snowflakes clinging to his eyebrows. Even in the dim glow of the headlights, I can see how pink his cheeks are. How blue his lips are turning. I must be in worse shape than even that.

"Look, I get it, okay?" he says eventually. "Really, I do. I wouldn't want my mom or sister-in-law riding in the car with some stranger, either. And I know you have no reason to trust me, and there's nothing I can do to prove that I'm not dangerous, but I promise you I'm not." He chews his bottom lip, thinking. "Where's your phone?"

My brows draw down. "What? Why?"

"Do you have a phone?" he asks, shoving his hands into his pockets with a full-body shiver. His teeth have begun to chatter.

"Is there anyone out there who doesn't?"

"Dial 9-1-1, and tell them you need a police officer to come and pick you up. Even if we don't have service, an emergency call should go through. If you do that, I'll leave you alone. I'll drive away and leave you to it. I swear." He puts his hands up in defeat. "I just need to know that I'm not leaving you to die. Can you do that for me?"

My stomach clenches at the idea of calling the police but also at the idea of being left alone in the dark again when I'm just becoming used to the light. "I'm not calling the police."

"Okay, fine. Then I will." He reaches into his pocket, retrieving his phone and setting to work.

"*Wait! Stop!*" I shout, lunging forward without thinking. My foot hits a patch of ice, and I'm thrown forward. My feet slide across the pavement as I brace myself for a fall. My arms swing in circles, trying to right myself. It happens both in painfully slow motion and all at once as I lose control entirely and fall forward. I squeeze my eyes shut as I slam into something much softer—and much closer—than the ground.

Him. When I open my eyes, my hands are on his

chest, my face inches from his collarbone. I jerk back. "Sorry."

"You okay?" he asks at the same time, extending a hand toward me.

"Don't call the police." I force the words out, the fear in my chest as cold as the frozen snow piling up at my feet.

He glances down at his phone, the screen's blue glow illuminating his face. "Why not?"

"Because I don't need them." A lie. Not the first, and it certainly won't be the last.

He sighs, running a shaking hand over his cheek. "Okay, look. I'm not going to stand out here and fight with you, nor am I going to risk getting frostbite over this. So, you have a few choices. You can get in the car and let me drive you somewhere while you warm up. I'll drop you off at the first gas station or store that we see the instant we have cell service so you can call for a ride." He pauses. "*Or* you can say no again, and I'll get in that car and leave you alone, but I'm going to call the police and let them know you're out here all by yourself in the cold and need help."

"There's no service," I remind him, my last bit of hope.

"I already said I don't think you need service to call 9-1-1." I can't tell if he's certain, and *I'm* definitely not certain. I don't think it's a risk I'm willing to take.

I look toward the woods, considering running into them, but I know what's waiting for me if I do. The snow is deeper there, the wind colder and stronger as it winds through the narrow gaps between the trees.

"You have three seconds to—"

"Fine," I say, not bothering to hide my frustration. "Whatever." I turn back toward his car, trudging across the wet pavement on my way to the passenger seat.

He doesn't say anything as I open the door. I test the locks, making sure the button works, and when I lock it, the locks don't completely disappear.

Maybe I've seen too many horror films. Can't be sure.

The car smells of fast food and men's cologne. I breathe through my mouth as I search for signs of danger. I open the glovebox but find nothing to worry about.

He sinks into the seat next to mine and cranks up the heat, rubbing his hands together and holding them out in front of the vents as if they were a campfire. He shivers, leaning over to grab the brown paper sack from my floorboard, and I stay as far away from him as I can, still standing just outside the door.

"Sorry about the mess. It's a thirteen-hour road trip." He tosses the bag in the back. "Oh shoot." As he leans over again, this time reaching behind my seat, my stomach lurches, convinced he's going for a weapon and that this is it, but instead, he picks up a men's coat— heavier than the one he's wearing. He holds it out to me. "I forgot I had this. Here. Come on, get in. It's not much, but it'll help you get warm faster." He nudges it toward me again, and finally, I sit down, slamming my door shut and draping the coat over my legs.

It's hard to maintain my anger as the first bit of heat hits my body, warming parts of me I thought I might never feel again. I turn my head toward the window, trying not to let him see me shiver. I'm too cold to argue. Too exhausted to say much of anything. As the heat fills the car, surrounding me like a warm blanket fresh from the dryer, I rest my head against the seat.

My eyes are heavy and threatening sleep, which I absolutely can't allow right now. If I let my guard down, even for a second, that could be all it takes. It could be what he's counting on.

He puts the car in drive, and we crawl forward—slowly at first as he tries to maneuver us back onto the road. I feel the car rattling across the piles of snow, shimmying and shaking on the shoulder until we're back out on the highway, though even there, it isn't much smoother. There aren't enough cars on the road to keep it clear, or any cars on the road for that matter.

The wipers move at full speed, a steady, rhythmic *weep weep, weep weep, weep weep* that could put me to sleep if the heat wasn't already trying its hardest to.

"You never told me your name," he says, filling the silence and reminding me I'm still in the car with a total stranger. A stranger that, for all I know, could be imagining how my skin will taste soon.

"I know."

I can practically feel his obnoxious grin without looking over. "Well, I'm Walker. I told you that, right?"

"Mm-hmm."

"Like the Texas Ranger."

"Cool."

He clicks his tongue, patting his thumbs on the steering wheel as if to music, though there is none playing. "Oh, I know! Can I try to *guess* your name?"

"Only if you'd told me yours is Prince Eric."

He snorts. "Do you have a pet crab hitching a ride with us that I don't know about?"

"Why? You going to call the police and tell them about it?" I snap back, cutting a glance at him.

He's quiet for a long while, staring straight ahead. When he finally breaks the silence, it's to say, "The storm's getting really bad."

I nod my head, my body starting to relax as the heat settles into my bones. "This isn't even the worst of it from what I've heard. More is coming soon. It's going to be a rough night."

"Yeah, I know. I was, um, I was hoping to outrun it," he mutters, his hands flexing on the steering wheel.

The *until your stubborn ass came along* isn't said aloud, but it's heavily implied.

"Are you not used to driving in this or something?"

"Not really. My family is from a few hours west of here, so we get snow, but not a ton. I live in South Carolina now, though. I try not to travel when there's snow, but I thought I could beat it here and got held up

14

by a few things instead." He eyes me. "What about you? Are you from this area?"

If he thinks this is going to be that easy, that I'm just going to open up and tell him my life story, he's wrong. I turn my head toward the window, staring out at the storm without a word.

"I drive through here on the way home sometimes. Whenever I don't fly, I mean. But I don't really like flying, you know? Not if I can help it. And especially not when I have all my bags and Christmas gifts for my nieces in the car. You can't trust airports not to lose everything these days, you kno—"

"How much longer until we get to town?"

He stops talking, deflating like a balloon. Quickly though, he seems to bounce back.

"An hour?" he grumbles, fiddling with the wipers, though they seem to be on the highest setting already. "Maybe more. Definitely more if the storm keeps up like this. What brings you to the middle of nowhere, Illinois, anyway?"

I don't look his way as I answer, squeezing my eyes shut as I feel a headache forming at the base of my skull. "Just needed to clear my head."

I lean forward and turn the radio up without asking, hoping to buy myself the rest of the ride in silence before I say something I'll regret.

CHAPTER TWO

WALKER

"Really? That's all I'm getting?" I ask, leaning forward to turn the radio back down as I stare at this strange, mysterious woman sitting in my passenger seat, who is still trying to pretend she's not shivering underneath my coat.

She folds her arms across her chest without looking my way. "It's the truth."

"So, let me get this straight. You needed to clear your head, so you decided to go for a walk down the interstate in the middle of the worst blizzard this area's seen in a long time?" I scoff. She's ridiculous and maddening. I should just ignore her, get her to where we're going in silence, and move on with my life, but I can't. I need to understand. "This was a choice you made?"

"That's correct." She closes her eyes, resting her head against the seat.

Slowing the car down as we come up to a patch of pavement that looks like ice, I maneuver us around it carefully before asking, "Where did you come from, then? Did you walk from your house? Or from a friend's house? Somewhere I can take you back to?"

"No."

"Do you or do you not live around here?"

She turns her head to stare at me. "How much longer are we going to play Twenty Questions?"

"As long as it takes for me to get some real answers out of you."

Facing forward again, she purses her lips. "Answers were never a part of the deal."

"Can you just—" I jolt as the car skids across a patch of ice, and it's as if I'm touching the ice with my body rather than the tires. My entire body is suddenly a shard of frozen water, breakable and still as I wait for the impact. Before I know what's happening, the car rights itself, staying steady on the road. I huff out a breath, hand to my chest. I really, really hate this weather.

Next to me, she's hardly flinched.

"Can you just give me something? Anything?" I demand, suddenly angrier than I expected to be. "A name? A... Hell, a business card? A carrier pigeon message? Something?"

Without warning, she slams her hands on either side of her and looks at me. "I was walking because I got in a fight with my boyfriend, and he kicked me out of the car. Is that what you want to hear?" she blurts out, all in one breath.

"What?"

The fact that she won't look at me tells me there's truth in her words, even if it's not the entire truth.

She folds her arms across her chest, slowly bobbing her head up and down. "Yeah, so...you'll excuse me if I don't feel like gabbing."

"He kicked you out in this storm?" I study her. She can't be more than a hundred and thirty pounds, a tiny little thing. This weather will kill her. I'm seeing red over this stranger, ready to fight for her. To confront this guy. "How long ago?"

"I don't know," she mumbles. "Half an hour or so."

"That's not much of a boyfriend," I manage to mutter, hardly breathing.

"Tell me something I don't know."

"He didn't come back for you? Or try to call you?"

She inhales sharply, adjusting in her seat. "Can we just move on from this? He's an asshole. Lesson learned."

"I'm sorry that happened to you, um..." I trail off, still not knowing what to call her.

"Tibby." She says a word I don't recognize, and I glance her way out of the corner of my eye.

"Gesundheit?" I offer playfully.

She rolls her eyes, sinking lower in her seat. "My name. It's Tibby."

"Oh. That's...different."

"Much like Walker, unless you're a country singer or Texas Ranger."

I snort at that, and to my surprise, she's smiling too,

but it's just for a brief second. As if she didn't realize she was doing it. Then, it's gone.

"It's short for Tabitha, after my grandmother."

"I like it. Tibby." I repeat the name, letting it roll off my tongue. Somehow, it fits her. It reminds me of a moody cat with its back arched, hair standing in every direction. Probably best not to say that, though.

"I'll be sure to let my mom know," she says under her breath, brushing the hair back from her face.

"So, where are you headed, Tibby?" I ask. "Where will you get a ride after I drop you off?"

"I'm not sure, really. We, um, we were driving to Chicago to visit his parents, but obviously I'm not going there now. I have some friends in St. Louis, so maybe I'll head there."

"St. Louis? Is that home for you?" I venture to ask, though I know it's probably too much.

"No. I don't know if I have a home anymore, really. I'm sort of...nomadic? I don't know if that's the right word. I move around a lot. Hotels, short-term rentals. I don't like to stay in one place too long."

"Well, that sort of makes you sound like a criminal," I tell her with a chuckle.

"I just don't like to be tied down. I grew up in a small town, and we never left. Not to travel, not for vacations. To this day, my dad has never slept on a bed that isn't his. He refuses. I hated it. I couldn't breathe, couldn't—" She stops as if she hadn't meant to go on like that. "It doesn't matter. I just hated it. I want to see as much of the world as I can."

In a strange way, I get it. I grew up in one place, and though I've gotten out and traveled, I've never truly left. Not in a way that matters. Home still feels like home, and I assume, someday, I'll end up back there. Just like my parents and their parents and so on. But then again, I think there's something to be said about building a home you love. Taking pride in where you're from.

"Well, for this portion of your tour of the world, allow me to be your tour guide. This is Interstate fifty-seven. Or, as I like to call it, just fifty-seven. A very important part of the world," I say, waving a hand toward the windshield. "Go on. Take it all in. I know the beauty of it must be truly astounding to you, but try to reign in your applause."

That gets a hint of a smirk, an upturned corner of her mouth. I'll take it.

The headlights land on a blue sign up ahead, telling us we're nearing the first rest area in miles.

"Do you mind stopping up here?" I ask. "I need some coffee to warm up. Looks like you could use some, too. Maybe they'll have a pay phone or something, and you could try to call someone?"

"Sure," she says, rubbing her hands over her arms.

The rest area comes within half a mile, and I slow us down, easing over. The car rattles with a steady *ch-ch-ch-ch-ch* on the exit ramp, which is packed with snow and ice. It might've been a bad idea to stop in a parking lot that looks as if they forgot to salt it, but if I don't get something to eat and drink soon, I'm worried I won't make it much farther.

I pull into the spot that looks the clearest, though none of them are particularly great, and shut off the car. The cold from outside immediately begins to seep in, even before we open the doors. It's as if the car has released a breath.

In front of us, there's a single building with roughly cut stone on its exterior. There's a warm amber light out front to make the entrance seem safe, but two vending machines behind metal bars contradict the appearance of any such safety.

"I'm going to the bathroom, then to get a snack. You want or need anything?" I look over at her while rubbing my hands together to keep them warm.

"No, thanks. I'll go look for a phone." She hesitates, obviously toying with saying something while my bladder burns for relief.

"What is it?"

"I, um..." Her dark brows pinch together in thought. "Should you just leave me here?"

I stare at her, somehow understanding that she's actually asking *if* I will leave her here. As if she doesn't want me to, but she can't admit it, even to herself.

"No." I check my phone. "The cell service is still shitty through here. If you find a pay phone and call someone, I'll leave you, if that's what you want. But if not, or if you don't want me to leave you... Tibby, you're welcome to ride with me as long as you'd like. There's no time limit here. Honestly, I'm happy for the company."

She stares as if she's trying to understand me—I can practically hear my mother's voice saying, *good luck with that*—then shakes her head. "Well, hopefully I'll find a phone and be out of your hair, but if not, thank you."

I want to tell her she's not in my hair and demand to know who has made her feel so afraid and unwanted, but I don't. We just met. We're strangers, and I don't want to overstep. Or scare her away.

Feral cat, I remind myself. She's a feral cat I've managed to lure a step closer to me. If I make any sudden moves, I'll cause her to retreat. To hiss and run away, maybe claw my eyes out in the process. I have to take my time with her.

I push open my door and step out, blasted by the icy wind. Snowflakes cling to my eyelashes, hair, and skin, and I turn my back to the wind, stepping up onto the sidewalk and making my way toward the building with her next to me.

The sidewalk, at least, has clearly been salted, though snow is still sticking to the grass on either side. We make it inside the building and part ways. She goes left, and I go right.

The building is cool and silent, filled with shelves of brochures about local attractions. In the center of the room, there's a round information desk, though no one is behind it. The lobby is dimly lit, but the hall to the bathroom is bright.

Inside, there's a condom dispenser on the wall and paper towels thrown carelessly on the floor. The mirror is smudged with specks of soap and God knows what else, and in the stall, there are posters about domestic abuse and human trafficking. I read all of the writing on the inside of the stall, anything to keep my mind from obsessing over her. She's a mystery, a giant question mark tied up in a little bow and suddenly thrust into my life, and I can't stop wanting to unravel her.

After I've used the restroom, I head back out into the lobby, where I locate two more vending machines in the building and pull out a few bills from my pocket. There's no coffee like I was hoping for, so I choose a Diet Dr Pepper and a bag of M&M's as I wait for her to return from the hall she disappeared down.

I should probably get something for her, I realize, after I've torn my bag of M&M's open. She didn't have a purse on her, so it's likely she doesn't have any money. I could wait to ask her what she prefers or to ask her if she's even hungry, but regardless of whether or not she is, I assume she'll deny it. She said she didn't want anything when I asked earlier, but I won't be able to eat and drink in front of her without feeling like a jerk, so I should probably pick something out and offer it to her just in case. If nothing else, I'll have extra for myself later.

Now, the hard question: what exactly does a feral cat like to eat? There's no milk. No meat.

I smile internally at my own joke, then decide just to ask her what she likes, rather than waste my money with guesses. I don't want to risk choosing something she hates or is allergic to, and if she couldn't eat it, having an extra snack while she has none would only make me feel guilty.

Asking is the easiest solution. We both know she has to be starving. I'll simply refuse to take no for an answer.

Just as soon as she comes out of the bathroom...

After a while, I start to worry that she's left already, and I missed her. I check the parking lot to be sure she didn't steal the car somehow, but to my relief, it's still there. Right where I left it.

Soft footsteps echo down the hall, and I look up, seeing her come into view. The first thing I notice is that she's dry, the calf-deep dampness from earlier now gone. She must've used the hand dryer to dry her clothing, which means, just minutes ago, it's possible she was standing half-naked in the bathroom a few feet from me.

What if someone had walked in?

What if someone had seen her?

What if... What if *I'd* walked in?

I swallow, looking down to shield myself from the possibility of her reading my thoughts somehow, then back up. "Any luck finding a phone?"

With her arms crossed, she shakes her head. "We should get going before we end up stuck here."

I follow her eyeline to the glass doors, where the storm seems to have gotten even worse outside. "We could stay," I say softly. "I mean, until things calm down. At least it's warm in here." I gesture to the vending machines. "We have food, water, and bathrooms. We could hang out until the storm calms down and then get back on the road."

She chews the inside of her cheek, drawing it inward, then shakes her head. "I can't stay here."

"What are you talking about?" It can't be that she's not okay with spending more time with me, surely, after she just asked to leave with me now. "Why not?"

"I just need to keep moving." Her eyes squeeze shut. "Look, I can't force you to come with me. Maybe it's not safe. But I can't stay here."

Something about the way she says it, the panicked look in her eyes, tells me she's running from something. And running fast.

"Just tell me one thing..."

She nods.

"Are you in danger? Or trouble? Is there a reason you need to keep moving when you've already said you have no idea where you're going?"

She swallows and drops her chin to her chest. When she looks back up, it's with a steely gaze. "Look, I can't make you do anything. But I'm leaving. I'm not wasting time on some little sleepover here."

"I never suggested—"

"Storm or no storm, I want to get to my family. Friends. I do not want to spend New Year's Day with some stranger I met on the interstate."

I try not to let the words sting. I shouldn't care, but I do. "Fair enough. I get that, but it's not safe. Wouldn't you rather be cautious and actually make it to them than try to go when it's dangerous and get hurt? Or worse..."

She heads for the door without pause. "I'll take my chances."

CHAPTER THREE

BEFORE

Snow makes this all so much easier.

I follow the footprints and trail of blood across the white ground like a hunter chasing a rabbit. Carefully. Methodically. Using my phone's flashlight to light the way. I don't even have to move quickly, really. He's too hurt to get far. Soon enough, he'll have expended all his energy. His body will give out. He'll collapse and wait for me to end it all, and that's exactly what I'll do. Happily.

So, while I wait, I play my favorite game. The one he's learning at the moment.

Hunter and prey.

At least, I have to assume this is what a hunter would do. I have no actual experience with the sport. Maybe they'd sic a dog on them instead, but I don't have a dog.

Just me.

And I haven't let myself down yet.

The footprints are deep and hurried, blurring

together in places where he tripped or stumbled—signs of the fast, panicked way he's traveling. Next to them, the thin trail of red specks paints the snow a brilliant shade of crimson. It's obvious from the way the blood is splattered in thin lines appearing to get thinner that he's running, trying to escape me, but it's no use.

I could've told him that if he'd listened.

But they never do...

Each one always thinks they're smarter than the last. Stronger than the ones who came before them. They always think they can get away or outsmart me, but they can't.

When I eventually find him, he's hiding next to a tree, cowering down like a puppy or small child waiting to be kicked. He's bleeding from the last hit, a swing of my shovel from the trunk when he was least expecting it. I caught him off guard, but then again, perhaps he should've helped me load the vehicle. If he had, he might've asked why I was loading a shovel and no bags into the car.

He looks up at me with a quivering bottom lip, though whether it's from fear or the cold, or a mix of both, I'm not totally sure. His hands go up, trying to shield himself from me.

"Please..." he whispers, trying to stand, his hand on the tree. "Please don't do this. You don't have to..." He's too weak to finish the sentence, let alone stand. He's lost too much blood from the stab wound in his stomach— the last thing I did before he began to run. He tried to call for help, too, I'm sure, but I waited until service dropped like I knew it would, like it always does through here. The blizzard just added to the problem—or, for me, the solution.

I raise the knife in my hands, my body buzzing with adrenaline over what I know is coming. This isn't my favorite part—the teasing and the torturing will always claim that spot—but this is when it all ends.

And endings, I've come to learn, are just as satisfying.

CHAPTER FOUR

TIBBY

"Hey! Hey, wait up!" he shouts after me, rushing to keep up as I push open the door and step out into the icy night. The wind howls, whipping my hair in every direction while I trudge down the sidewalk. Ice crunches beneath my boots on the way to the car.

When we reach the parking lot, he picks up speed to cut me off. "Will you just hold on a minute, you stubborn ass?"

I stop in my tracks, a grin playing on my lips. "Did you just call me a stubborn ass?"

His eyes dance between mine, trying to read me. "Well, you are, aren't you?"

"Proudly," I confirm. "But that doesn't mean I'm okay with you calling me out on it."

He sighs, a hand to his chest as he catches his breath. "I'm not saying I won't go with you. I was just throwing out options. If you would just talk to me, we could make a joint decision."

"I don't need to talk to you, and our decisions shouldn't be joint. *My* decision is made. You don't feel safe, so clearly your decision is made, too. It's honestly not a big deal. You got me so much farther already. I can make it the rest of the way." I pat his chest, moving past him. "You're off the hook, Walker."

"The rest of the way to where?" he demands, turning around carefully on the icy lot to watch as I walk away. "Where are you even going?"

I glance over my shoulder, slowing down only slightly. "Carbondale, I guess. Or Marion. As soon as I'm in town, as soon as I have service or find a pay phone, I'll call a friend and have her come pick me up." I pause, turning to face him once more. "I'll be okay. I dried off. I'm warm. I'm much safer now than I was before, so thank you. But I'm honestly going to be fine now. My friend will get me."

He shakes his head, staring around at the snow as it whips past us. "And what if she can't get out in this? You'll be stranded and alone in the storm. Is that really what you want?"

"The roads will be clear in town." It would be easy enough to stay here, obviously, but I can't. I have to keep moving. I have to find a way to call...someone. Jess, maybe. Or my parents, though God knows what that phone call will be like.

"You know that for sure? Southern Illinois is a different world than Chicago. They don't keep their roads clear here. The cities shut down over a dusting of snow. It's not safe. And I don't just mean the roads for *us*. I'm saying if something happens, I'm not sure the police or an ambulance could get to us either. We'd be totally stranded and alone and potentially hurt if we had a wreck. If the car was totaled, we'd be without heat. For hours, days maybe. It's not safe," he repeats slowly as if hoping I'll comprehend.

"Well..." I cross my arms. He's right. I don't know this area. I only know it from passing through on my way to St. Louis or the two trips I've taken to Chicago with Craig, and I never paid much attention to these quiet little towns. "Okay, fine. What are you suggesting, then? We stay here and wait out the storm? What if the storm gets worse, and we're stuck here for days?"

"That shouldn't happen, but if it does, don't you think it would be better to be here than there?"

I think about it for a moment. Staying in one place feels dangerous right now. Risky. But I do understand what he's saying. Much like with the decision to ride with him in the first place, I have to weigh the options in my head and decide which carries the most hope. Here, we're safe, but there's no hope of making it farther. Of getting out. Of contacting anyone. If we try, at least there's a chance. Right now, we haven't even had any close calls. It still feels like it's worth the risk to me.

"I can't stay here, Walker. I'm sorry."

He massages his forehead with both hands, wincing.

When he drops them, he says, "Okay, fine. We can keep driving." He checks over his shoulder, surveying the storm. "We just... We'll have to take it slow."

"Like we were before. We'll be fine."

He doesn't seem so sure, but he uses his key fob to unlock the car anyway and pulls open his door. Back inside the vehicle, he turns on the heat. We sit and idle for a moment, giving the car a chance to warm up.

"How much gas do you have?" I ask, leaning over to get a better view.

"Enough for now. I stopped a while back. We should be okay to make it to Marion."

The windshield is already coated in a thick layer of snow, but I'm relieved to see there's at least no ice this time. The storm is changing. More puffy snow, less ice. A good sign.

We're going to be okay.

"If we can make it to Marion," he goes on, "I'll stop at a hotel for the night. You're welcome to stay, too, if you want." I cut a glance his way, and he quickly adds, "I'll cover the cost to get you a separate room if you can't pay for it, obviously."

I bristle at his words. "I don't need your charity."

"Fine then, you can get yourself a room."

"I don't need a room."

"You don't need much, do you, Tibby?" he asks with a wry expression, his eyes pinched like he's trying to read me. Unfortunately for him, I'm practiced in the art of keeping my face blank. Unreadable.

"Where are *you* headed, anyway?" I ask. "Why are you here right now?"

"Well, let's see…" He taps his chin. "I'm here right now because I've had three coffees today, and my bladder was bursting."

"Ha-ha, Walker. You really missed your calling in comedy."

"Who says I'm not a comedian?" he teases, finally putting the car in reverse and backing out.

"Well, clearly not at Kevin Hart's level yet," I reply, running a finger over the peeling leather of my seat.

"Don't hate on Annie." He narrows his eyes at me, a playful hint to them.

"Annie?"

"As in little orphan…" He pats his head.

"The red hair. Got it." I nod, then roll my eyes as I turn my head away from him. "Of course you named your car."

He laughs. "Why?"

"You just have that personality."

"I don't know whether or not to be offended." We pick up speed as we ease back out onto the interstate.

"I just mean you've got that free-spirited, happy-go-lucky personality."

"What makes you say that?"

"You picked up a stranger on the interstate and never once questioned if I could be a serial killer, for one thing."

He nudges me gently with his elbow. "You don't

exactly look the type." He's quiet for a moment. "And anyway, I know you think you've got me all figured out, but I promise you don't. Maybe I'm just letting you think I'm this nice and carefree."

I shrug. No one's that good an actor, but I decide not to press the issue. Just then, the first vehicle I've seen all night speeds past us—a white car going way too fast for the road conditions.

"I guess if you'd waited a while longer, you could've gotten a ride with them. They certainly seem to be in a hurry. More your speed." He gestures toward them.

"Nah, clearly they would've been in such a hurry they wouldn't have stopped anyway. You know, like normal people. Didn't your parents ever teach you not to talk to strangers?" I scowl at him.

"Well, you'd have had an easier evening than spending time with me, I guess. Just think, you could still be miles back, just the snow and ice to keep you company, freezing your stubborn ass off."

"You sure like bringing up my ass," I say, not realizing the words are coming out of my mouth until they have.

He barks out a laugh, then gives me a side-eye that's meant to be flirtatious, I'm sure. "Well..." He gives another laugh. "No, never mind. I'm not going to be a creep on this trip, I swear."

"I appreciate it." Adjusting in the seat, I point out, "You never answered my question, by the way."

"What question?"

"About why you're here."

"Oh. I'm going to St. Louis, actually. That's where my parents are from. Well, a small little town outside of it that no one's ever heard of. Going home for the new year."

I eye him. "St. Louis? I thought you called yourself a *southern gentleman* earlier. You mean to tell me you're actually from the Midwest?"

He snorts, glancing at me with a wry twist of his lips. "Yeah, go ahead and try to convince my mom we aren't southern. You're both stubborn as they come, so something tells me it'd be an argument to watch."

I purse my lips to hide my grin. "You didn't make it home for Christmas, then?"

"No, I had to work. New Year's is our tradition. It's when my brother and sister-in-law can visit, too, so it works out." He bobs his head up and down slowly as if making a silent decision. "You mentioned St. Louis earlier, didn't you? You have friends there?"

I nod. "Yeah, a few who I went to high school with. We've stayed in touch."

"Well, if it makes it any easier on you or them, you're welcome to ride all the way there if you want. That way your friends don't have to come so far. I can drop you off on the outskirts of the city if they'll meet us."

It's a generous offer. One he has no reason to make, which has me immediately suspicious.

Something about this whole scenario is too good to be true. No one is this nice.

"Thanks. I'll think about it."

"Okay, cool." He reaches forward and turns up the radio. A Post Malone song comes on, and I close my eyes, drowning out all thoughts to the sound of it, waiting for any sign that we're nearing civilization. When the song ends, I open my eyes again, staring out the window at the storm as it rages around us.

Out here like this, it's easy to feel like nothing else exists.

Just us, the road, and the darkness.

CHAPTER FIVE

WALKER

After a few moments, she leans forward, holding her hands in front of the vent to warm them.

"You can point some of my vents at you if you're still cold," I say, adjusting the one closest to her to help.

"I'm okay. It's just my fingers."

"I wish I had gloves in here, but I don't."

"Yeah, well, you'd think I would've brought some, but the only ones I had were in my bag, and..." She sighs. "Obviously, I don't have that anymore."

"Do you think you'll talk to him again?"

"Who? My boyfriend?"

I try not to be affected by the word, though I hate that she still calls him that after what he did.

"I don't know. I mean, I guess at some point I'll have to, won't I? At least to get my things back."

When I look over, she's still fiddling with her own

vents, and I notice something staining the sleeve of her jacket. Something dark.

"Is that blood?" I cry, taking my eyes off the road for a second to stare at it. "Are you hurt?"

She twists the sleeve to look at it, running her finger over the stain with a strange expression. Then she turns it quickly until it's under her wrist, and I can no longer see it, but I didn't miss the fact that her hands have scrapes and blood on them as well. "No. I'm fine."

"Are you sure? That looks like blood. Your hands look rough."

She doesn't look at me, and I suddenly have an inkling about why she's in such a hurry and why she doesn't want to talk about her boyfriend. Red fury ignites in me like a wick lit on fire. "Did he hurt you when you fought? Tell me the truth."

She shakes her head, but it's halfhearted. "I'm fine, Walker. I'm a big girl. I've been taking care of myself a long time."

I wring my hands around the steering wheel, imagining it's his neck. "You should go to the police. Tibby, you should go to the police right now. Immediately. You have to make sure he can never hurt you again. Does he know where you live?"

She stares straight ahead, not answering, which I take to mean that he does.

"Tibby, if he knows where you live, he could find you if you go home or... Well, I know you said you don't have a permanent home, but he'll know where to look for you, won't he? He knows where you're staying. Or where you might stay. He'll come after you and...he could really hurt you."

She tucks her hands under her legs, leaning back in her seat. "I'm fine, Walker. Honestly. It's not worth the headache, trust me. He's not coming after me. He's long gone."

I don't like the answer, but with no real right to say anything, I let it go.

"Are you close with your parents?" she asks, changing the subject with razor-sharp focus.

"Yeah, I guess so. I mean, they're my parents, you know? So we have our little disagreements, but for the most part, they're pretty cool."

"And your brother?"

"Yeah. We're only a year apart in age, so we were close growing up and have gotten closer now. He lives in Utah, though. Salt Lake City. So I don't see him too often. Just the holidays."

"So you were heading home to visit them? Am I slowing you down?" she asks, with a hint of vulnerability that stings me to my core.

I swallow. "Only if you're the one in charge of this storm."

To that, she finally laughs. "Nope, I can't say that I am."

"Didn't think so. What about you? Do you have siblings?"

"Nope. It's just me and my parents."

"And you're close? Or no?"

She adjusts in her seat, tugging at the sleeves of her shirt as she seems to search for the answer. "Um... Well, not particularly, no. We aren't, like, mortal enemies or anything. They're my parents, you know? But we aren't close. They don't agree with most of my life choices, and they've made that super clear. They wanted me to settle down, have kids, live near them. Basically everything I didn't do. And, when I'm not doing what they want me to do, everything between us is strained. And I'm to blame for it all."

"So...you don't want to settle down? Have kids? Not in the cards for ya?"

"I don't know. Someday, maybe. Not right now, at least. I like being wild right now. Free. It's not like you get a do-over for these years. You don't get the time back...being young, you know? I can't be sixty and decide to abandon my family because what I'd like more than anything else is to finally take some desperately needed alone time."

"Sure you can," I say, though I know what she means. "But it's harder. I get it."

"Yeah, it's just...I know they're happy, but I want...I want something more for my life. I want to see the world and try new things and chase my dreams. They think that's all silly and dangerous." She releases a long exhale. "Plus, they hated my ex."

I look over at her out of the corner of my eye. "You mean the guy from tonight?"

She nods. "Craig."

"Well, I can't say I don't agree with their feelings about Craig, but I thought you called him your boyfriend earlier? Is he an ex?"

She pauses for several seconds, and I can practically hear her thinking. "I don't know what he is. It was kind of a dramatic exit if I'm being honest. But I'm done with him, so I guess so." Twisting a piece of her hair, she looks up at me. "He wasn't a terrible boyfriend. Just selfish. And with a temper."

"Sounds like a recipe for disaster."

"Well, I've never been very good in the kitchen. Recipes aren't exactly my thing." She runs a hand over her face, yawning as I smirk.

"You can sleep, you know. If you're tired. I'll wake you when we get to a hotel."

She's quiet, and I know she won't accept the offer, but I had to make it anyway. "Thanks."

"No problem..." I slow my words as something up ahead catches my eye. Easing my foot onto the brake pedal, I lean closer to the windshield to get a better look. "What the..."

"What's that?" She leans forward, too, hands clasped in her lap, the horror of the situation clear in her voice.

"Maybe there was an accident." My throat is suddenly too dry. "Or the roads are really bad. Either way, we aren't getting through."

Ahead, there's an orange-and-white blockade in the center of the interstate with several flashing cones and a warning.

ROAD CLOSED

CHAPTER SIX

BEFORE

I take it back. Everything I said before.

Snow didn't make this easier. Not at all.

Sure, it made the actual hunting easier. The finding. The killing.

But the cleanup? What a mess.

The snow across the forest floor is covered in his blood. Everywhere I look, even with the sky now dark and everything cloaked in shadows, there's red. Dark patches against the brilliant-white blanket of snow.

His body is gone. That part I handled, though the snow made that part more difficult, too. Digging a grave in frozen earth? Not for the weak, let me tell ya.

My hands are bloody and blistered, and my arms and back still ache from the exertion of trying. I feel as if I've been hit by a truck, and my work still isn't done. In the end, I gave up when I had to. Thanks to the sounds of a pack of coyotes nearby—noises that normally would've sent chills down my spine but this time filled me with hope and relief like I've never known—I came up with a new, better idea. After carefully separating the parts of his body that I was able to, I dropped chunks of him here and there. Practically a fine-art display, if I'm being honest. Something beautiful and real and raw like I've never seen. I scattered him like feed, leaving a delicious trail of dinner for the animals, my thanks for their help cleaning up my mess. With all that blood, it won't be long before they've found him and gotten rid of him, but now, what am I supposed to do with this mess from the killing and dismembering itself? How am I supposed to clean it up? And how much longer do I have?

In the middle of nowhere, the chances of anyone finding any part of his body or stumbling into this bloody crime scene before the snow melts is slim, but there's still a chance, and I can't discount that. Thinking ahead, planning, knowing when to play what role and for how long is what's gotten me here. It's how I've come this far. If I left everything up to fate and hoped for the best, I would've been caught several times by now.

I'm a firm believer in planning everything, which is probably why I'm feeling out of sorts with this one. It's the first time I've killed someone and let my emotions get involved. Let myself get sloppy. If I'd been smart, I would've waited for spring or summer. And I certainly would've come up with a plan that didn't leave his car a few miles back, abandoned on the side of the road just waiting to be found.

A plan that would've involved me having a way out of here, because there's no way in hell I'm getting back into his car for multiple reasons, but mostly because, if I'm caught, it will look so much worse.

Sorry, Officer, I have no idea where he is. I just borrowed his car.

When someone reports him as missing, they'll make him out to be a saint. A god among men. They'll sing his praises and speak about what an amazing man he was, what a monster someone would have to be to take him away from the ones who loved him.

It's what always happens. The price I pay for ridding the world of men like him. I'll spend the rest of my life hearing about how amazing they were. In death, everyone becomes a hero. Otherworldly. The dead become something of myths and legends, even when everyone knows the truth.

Everyone in his life must know what a stain on society he is, but now that he's gone, it'll all be forgotten. Forgiven. He'll be immortalized and remembered only for his best moments.

But not by me. I will make it my life's mission to remember him for the bad.

If he'd been different, he'd still be alive.

If he wasn't the person he was, I wouldn't be soaked in his blood right now. I took off my outer layer of clothing and used it to dress his body so it'll be destroyed along with every piece of him, but still, there are specks of blood that remain. Evidence of everything that happened. Splatters in my hair, on my jacket, under my fingernails.

Proof of what I've done if someone wants to look hard enough.

I move through the snow, dusting it apart carefully, throwing handfuls this way and that. The knife stays with me in my pocket always. It's the only thing that could tie the murders to me if they wanted to. And so, it must stay.

I hear a noise and freeze. In the silence of the snowy night, a car is growing closer. I drop the handful of snow, looking around.

I haven't seen one in hours. Not since we stopped earlier. *Who in the world is stupid enough to be out in this storm?*

For a while, worry overtakes me. If they see his car, they might try to stop or call the police. If they do that, there's a good chance I'll be caught.

Then again, once I've had a moment to process my fear, I realize this could be a good thing. After all, I was just thinking about how I'll need a car, wasn't I? I can't take his, and with this storm, walking seems like a nightmare. I bend at the waist and dust myself off, cleaning the last remaining evidence away as much as I'm able to.

Then, I head for the road and for the car I hear drawing closer with every second. I know what they'll think of me upon first sight. That I'm out here alone and helpless.

It's a superpower, in a way. Looking innocent when you're anything but.

Here goes nothing.

CHAPTER SEVEN

TIBBY

With the road up ahead closed, we have no choice but to veer off at the last available exit. It's desolate and dark, with no signs of gas or places to stay. It would've been my last choice had I been given one, but I haven't.

Immediately, I realize what a mistake this was. If we thought the interstate was bad, this road is by far much worse. The highway is long and empty, stretching on for miles with snow-covered woods on either side. There are no houses or stores. No cars. Nothing to let us know the world hasn't ended and forgotten about us here on this dismal stretch of earth.

We drive much slower here. It seems darker somehow, the road conditions much icier. Every few miles, we hit a patch of thick snow, jogging the car forward or slowing it down, and my heart rises in my throat.

I hate this weather.

And, if something happens to us, I'll have to live with

the fact that it'll be all my fault. If I live, I guess. If I make it through any of this.

"Where are we even going?" I ask. Snow whips through the air with increasing speed, the headlights illuminating the falling flakes against the dark sky.

"I have no idea." He presses the button to turn on the defrost as the windows fog over. "There was nothing on the sign that said a town name or anything, was there? Only something about Marion, but we're still several miles from there. Hopefully we'll be able to find a detour to take us back to the interstate. I should really pull off and figure it out, but I doubt there's service yet and I'm scared the car will get stuck on the shoulder." At once, both of us study the snow built up on the shoulders, and I can't help agreeing with him. He nods in my direction. "Can you try to pull up a map on your phone? See if there's service here?"

I hesitate, glancing down at my pocket. "There won't be."

"How do you know?"

"Well, because why would there be more service here when the storm isn't any better?"

"We're at least a little closer to the city, I think. There's rarely service out the way we came from, even when the weather's good." He glances over at me, clearly suspicious. "Is there a reason you don't want to check it? Is your phone turned off so he can't track you?"

I chew my bottom lip, weighing my options, limited

as they are. "I don't have a phone," I say eventually. "I lost it in the fight. It's not a big deal."

"Seriously?"

"Mm-hmm."

His lips pinch together in thought. "Why did you lie to me when I asked earlier?"

"I didn't lie. You asked if I had a phone, and I asked if you know anyone who doesn't. Not a lie. A question."

His eyes cut to me with clear annoyance. "Clever."

I wrinkle my nose at him. "I didn't want to admit I don't have one. Not because I'm embarrassed about it or anything, but because..." I stop, catching myself.

He exhales slowly, as if he's figured it out. "Because you didn't want me to know you wouldn't be able to call for help."

The words chill my skin as I nod. I still don't want him to know, if I'm being honest, but I don't see that I had a choice but to tell him.

He inhales. "Okay, let's make a pact."

"Okay..." I draw out the word.

"No lies to each other while we're traveling together. You can ask me anything, and I'll be honest with you. Not like lifelong hidden secrets, but things that we need to know to keep each other safe. And you won't lie to me, either. Deal?"

"Again, I didn't lie."

"That's not an answer."

"Fine, I won't lie to you. But now I feel like you have some hidden secrets you don't want to share with me."

He points up ahead. "Hey, look! I think there's a motel coming up. It's probably not much, but it'll do for the night and get us off the road. If I still don't have service here, and you don't want to stay, you can use one of the phones in the room to call someone. Although, if we can't get there, there's a good chance no one can get here, either. We might be stuck here for the night."

"What? No. We're stopping? I thought you said we could get to Marion from here. We have to keep going, keep trying. We're doing fine."

The car jerks forward, sliding as we hit another patch of ice as if trying to prove me wrong.

He slows the car down even further, holding the steering wheel with a vise-like grip. "I don't think it's safe to keep going. Especially not if we're having to avoid the interstate and take backroads." He fiddles with the defrost again, turning it up even more. "I'm sorry. I swear I'll take you to St. Louis just as soon as road conditions are safe. We'll pull over, get warm, then you can call your friend and at least let them know where you are. And we'll go from there. What do you say?"

I rest my tongue against my teeth. "I don't know."

The building comes into view up ahead, a small road-side motel with a glowing "Vacancy" sign and two cars in the parking lot. The building is red with eight white doors and windows and a concrete, covered walkway outside them, illuminated by small porch lights outside each door.

"We have to stop," he informs me. "I'm sorry. I've

taken you as far as I can tonight. Let's just go inside and call your friend, and you'll feel better. There's honestly no other choice. Walking now will take you even longer without the ability to walk the interstate. And, without a map, you'd end up lost. Just...come on. Rest for the night. Shower. Warm up. We'll figure everything else out tomorrow."

As much as I want to argue some more, to tell him he's giving up and demand we keep moving, I know he's right—though I'd never admit that to him. To drive any farther tonight with no idea where we're going or how much worse the roads will be is foolish. We'll end up hurt or dead.

I puff out a breath, pinching the skin around my wrist. "Okay, fine. Yeah."

"Awesome." He slows down as we near the motel, easing into the small parking lot on the corner of a four-way stop. There are no houses around. No businesses. Just this tiny motel and the woods. Across the street, there's another lot that I imagine could be used for additional parking, though with just eight rooms, I don't see how it would be necessary.

It's impossible to tell if the parking spaces are marked underneath all the snow, so I have no idea if we're in an official spot as we come to a stop in front of the office. Walker pushes open his door and eases out of the car without hesitation.

"Watch your step," he warns, gripping onto the hood of the car as he makes his way toward the front. I step out, following him cautiously. As we walk, I discover the parking lot is slick with random patches of ice underneath the snow, and I can only imagine how much a fall would hurt.

We make it to the front door and then inside the building. The small lobby is the size of an average kitchen. Its yellowing, laminate floors and cherrywood desk tell of its age. The fluorescent lights buzz overhead, giving everything a sickly yellow glow. The boxy, old computer on the desk has a dark screen, and as I look around, I realize there's no one here.

A single bell on the desk sits next to a sign that reads **Ring for Service.**

Walker looks at me, a brow quirked. It feels like we've walked onto the set of a horror movie. Everything is too quiet, too strange. He outstretches a finger and rings the bell with a soft *ching!*

Stepping back, he moves next to me, hands folded in front of him as he waits.

And waits.

And waits.

Several minutes pass with the incessant buzzing above our heads—the weird, disorienting glow of the lights making the room feel hazy and strange—before we hear a door open from somewhere down the hall, and then there's a set of footsteps moving slowly our way.

I swallow, turning my full body toward the sound, preparing for whoever might be coming.

A man pops his head around the corner, his gray hair

standing in every direction as if we might've woken him up. He runs a hand over his white, coffee-stained beard.

"I thought I heard something out here," he grumbles, more to himself than to us it seems like.

Slowly, he shuffles forward, making his way down the hall and behind the desk before he looks up at us with a long inhale. "What can I do for you, kids?"

I look up at Walker, trying to decide if I should be insulted. I'm in my thirties, and I'd guess he is, too. Hardly kids, if you ask me.

Walker clears his throat, resting both hands on the wooden desk. "Um, we need to book a room."

The man's eyes bounce to me with a gleam that tells me he thinks this is something it certainly isn't.

"You kids from around here?"

"Just passing through on our way to St. Louis," Walker answers before I can. "They have the interstate closed down on the way to Marion, so we had to pull off. We weren't sure there was anything out here, honestly."

"That's what happened to the others," he says, pointing at nothing. "Storm's turning out to be the best thing that ever happened to me. Ain't seen business like this in a decade or more."

Walker stares around the room, his eyes traveling over the mounted deer heads and a framed photograph of the man and a woman in front of the motel. "Yeah, I imagine it's slow around here."

"Wasn't always this way. We used to be fully booked most nights. But now, well, everything's moved to the city. The mines are shutting down left and right. People can't afford to stay here, and they're taking their businesses with 'em. The people who run this town are more worried about padding their pockets than helping the people who elected them." The man stops talking and taps his mouse, waiting for the computer to wake. "You said one room or two?"

Walker looks at me. "Are you planning on staying or...?"

"No," I say quickly. "My friend will come." I have no idea if that's true, but I hope so. I need to get out of here.

I'm not sure if it's just my imagination, but I could swear his face falls as I say it. Without missing a beat, though, he turns to the man, holding up a finger. "Just one for now. That may change depending on how things go."

The man nods, typing something into the computer. "I'll put you in room six, then. Room five is open next to it if you end up needing it. It's a hundred and nine a night." When Walker holds out a credit card, the man waves it away with a grim look. "Cash only, I'm afraid. The storm has wiped our whole system out."

"Oh, okay. No problem." Walker pulls out his wallet and hands him two hundred-dollar bills. I can't help noticing he has a lot of cash on him.

The man collects his change from the drawer, counting it back to him, then grabs an actual metal key from the wall behind him and hands it over. "If you lose this, it's fifty bucks to replace it, so don't lose it."

Walker takes the key, tapping it to his forehead with a salute. "You got it."

"Coffee's in the rooms, but you may want to grab some extra if you're a big drinker." He points to a small table with packs of coffee, cream, and sugar to the right of the desk. "Should be plenty of towels, but let me know if you need more." He sighs, scratching his head. "What am I forgetting here? Ah, right. Um, TVs are hit or miss tonight with the storm, so don't come tellin' me. You ain't tellin' me nothin' I don't know. There's an extra blanket in the closet. Might be musty. Hasn't been washed since the room was last used, which was a while ago. But it's clean. No delivery around here, especially not in this. There's a Dollar General up the road, but no guarantees they haven't closed. Twenty minutes to a restaurant, so I hope ya ain't hungry. Hm...I think that's it. If you need anything else, just ring the bell. My name's Ernest. Ernie. Sometimes I'm asleep, so you might have to ring it a few times."

"Is it just you here?" Walker asks. "Running the place, I mean."

The man looks shocked by the question, as if he's never been asked before. Then, his expression warms slightly, and he leans forward on the counter. "My wife and I bought this place in the late seventies. Different time. Different world. She got sick around a decade ago. She's still here, still fighting, but the motel's on me now. You'll see her out here in the morning for breakfast if you come in. We have cereal, nothing special, but she likes seeing the guests. Always has. We live in the back." He juts a thumb over his shoulder. "I always think about shutting it down, getting us a little apartment in town or something, but she loves it here. So, I figure, as long as she's with me, I'll keep this place going for nights like this. But most days, it's just the two of us around here."

"Wow," Walker says. "I'm so sorry to hear that. It must be hard."

"Shit happens, kid," the man says with a shrug. "Have a nice night. Checkout's around noon. I'll have cereal and milk out on the table around six. Might make up a pot of coffee, too, if you'd like." He pauses long enough for Walker to nod. "Coffee it is, then. Let me know if you need anything or decide to stay longer. This area out here will be one of the last to get plowed. City ain't worried about us."

"That's it? Do you need my ID or something?" Walker's brows draw down. "Or a credit card to put on file? Shouldn't I sign something?"

The man smirks as if it's a funny concept. "Like I said, the storm knocked our system out, and our copier's been out for a few months, so I guess we're working on the honor system tonight, kids. That okay?"

Walker nods. "Yeah, of course."

"Just don't leave me hanging, okay? And don't lose that key." He wags a finger at us.

"No, sir," Walker says, waving at the man as he turns to walk away and putting a hand out to let me lead us out the door. At the car, he goes to the back seat and pulls out a suitcase before leading us toward room six.

The room is bigger than I expected it to be, with two beds against the wall to our right and an old box television on the dresser to our left. The room smells stale, and when Walker places his suitcase on the bed, dust particles fly through the air.

"I'm going to take a shower," he says, running a hand over his eyes sleepily. "Give you some space to call your friend. Do you need anything?"

"I'm good," I say, crossing the room to approach the tan phone on the nightstand between the beds. Jess's phone number is one of the only ones I have memorized, and I already know she's not going to answer an unknown number. I just have to hope she sees the voicemail I'll leave and calls back soon.

Walker disappears into the bathroom, and seconds later, I hear the shower. Then, with a breath, I lift the phone to my ear and wait for the dial tone.

Nothing.

I look at the phone, then press it to my ear again. *Come on. Come on. Come on.*

Nothing happens.

I press the switchhook twice, staring at the phone in horror.

You've got to be fucking kidding me.

CHAPTER EIGHT

WALKER

Hot water has never felt so good.

I melt into it.

Allow it to melt into me.

Close my eyes and sink into the heat. The blissful, beautiful, life-altering heat.

It's magical. Madness. Beautiful. Everything all at once.

I stand in the water, not washing my body or daring to move. I can't. I just need to stand here, stand still, and feel. Exist.

It wasn't until the moment the scalding water hit my skin that I realized just how chilled to the bone I was. My toes are bright red, along with my knees and ankles. From the heat of the water, the rest of me is quickly becoming just as red.

I form a cup with my hands in front of my chest,

collecting the water in handfuls and dropping them down over myself.

As my body finds a normal temperature and the initial euphoria of the warmth wears off, I begin to form rational thoughts again.

And, not surprisingly, my first thoughts are of her.

I try to convince myself it's because she's a stranger in my room. A stranger who has taken over my night, who is grumpy and ungrateful, and without whom I might've made it farther than I did, might've passed through the closed interstate before whatever happened to close it occurred.

But I know it's not the whole truth.

For some inexplicable reason, this woman fascinates me. For all her stubbornness, her rage, her inability to answer a question, I can't help wanting to spend time with her. Wanting to know her better. Ask one more question.

As terrible as it sounds, as much of an ass as it makes me, I can't help the quiet voice in the back of my head that seems to be hoping her friend won't make it tonight. That she'll have to stay. That she might stay in this room with me for another hour or so, talk to me more, fight with me, even.

Maybe I have frostbite to the brain. Honestly, it's the only logical explanation.

I also—and this is the more rational side of my brain, thankfully, *glad to know it's still in there*—wonder who she is. Did she lie about that? Why was she running? Who is this mysterious man who hurt her? Is it his blood on her shirt? Or hers? Maybe someone else's entirely?

There are so many mysteries surrounding her. So many questions left unanswered.

I can't imagine what my parents would think of what I'm doing, but I'm sure they wouldn't be pleased. Don't leave her alone on the highway, sure, but to pick her up and bring her to a motel with me? I'm not sure they'd advise that I go this far.

I can't help thinking of Ernest and his wife, wondering what life must be like for them out here. Alone. For the last year, I've been alone. With friends, at times. But ever since Alicia and I broke up, I've kept my nose down, grinding at work. I never downloaded my old dating apps again or took my friends up on the offers to be set up. Maybe it's because I wanted to give myself time to get over the girl I thought I might marry someday, or maybe it's because I don't know what I want in life anymore.

Part of me has always thought I'd end up back home, that I'd settle down like my parents, and like Ernest, but another part has always craved the adventure Tibby talked about earlier.

There's this road I take to work every morning, and on it, I pass two houses, side by side. One is an older farmhouse with a classic wraparound porch, shutters, and character. The other is completely modern. Clean. It has black siding and large windows. They're so completely opposite, and yet I can picture living my life happily in either one. Two different lives, two different paths. In one, it's a quiet life. A wife. Two kids. A dog. We drink coffee on the porch together each evening and soak up the sunset. Christmases are cozy at our house, and we're the hosts for every family party.

The other is a bachelor life with all the amenities. I work my way up in the company, earn a great salary, and have my suits dry-cleaned. I'm happy alone. I watch what I want and do what I want. My house is always clean. There are no pets or sticky handprints to clean. It's not empty or lonely but fulfilling.

I see both options so clearly, and most days, I just wish someone would tell me which one to choose.

Today, Tibby is like that second house. Here I was thinking I had my life figured out. That I was happy. Fulfilled. Then she came along, and now I don't know anything except that I want to get to know her more.

When the hot water starts to run out, I shut it off, shivering instantly as I pull the curtain back and step onto the thin rug on the tile floor.

The small bathroom is filled with steam, rising up toward the yellow ceiling. I reach across the maroon counter to wipe the filmy mirror clean, getting a better look at myself.

I should've brought my suitcase in here, I realize, and it was honestly nothing but pure desire to be in hot water that made me forget. I wrap a towel around my waist, then run a hand over my hair and pull open the door.

I stick my head out into the room, and my heart drops when I realize it's empty.

She's gone.

I cross the room quickly, hoping to check out the window and catch her. I shouldn't have left her. If she tries to walk in this storm—and God knows she's stubborn enough to do it—it'll be a death sentence.

"What're you doing?"

I spin around at the sound of her voice to find her on the floor near the side of the bed, propped up on her hands and knees, staring at me like I've grown a second head.

I look down at myself, realizing what I must look like racing across the room in nothing but a towel. But she's still here, and somehow that makes it all okay.

Trying to regain my composure, I stare at her. "I could ask you the same thing."

She eases backward and sits on her heels, staring at me. "The phones don't work."

"What do you mean?" I shoot a glance at the phone, which is currently in its place on the end table.

"It's dead. There's no dial tone or anything. Just... nothing. I was trying to see if the phone line was unhooked or something."

"And?"

She shakes her head. "It's attached to the jack. The storm must've knocked out the phone lines, too."

"But not the power?" I run another hand over my hair, thinking. "That doesn't make much sense, does it?"

At least this means she'll have to stay, but I don't want it like this. It's terrible, the way she's looking at me.

"I'm not sure," she mutters. "Did you check your phone?"

I nod, gesturing toward the bathroom where it's still resting in my pants pocket, with less than ten percent battery left. "Yeah, still nothing. The storm must've taken out a tower. Actually, thanks for the reminder. I need to charge my phone before it dies." I grab my bag and place it on the bed, searching for my charger. When I find it, I gather a change of clothes before looking up at her and noticing the wary look on her face.

She swallows, looking bitter and angry but also somehow on the verge of tears.

"Hey, you're okay, you know? It's going to be okay. In the morning, we'll get back out on the road again. They'll have things cleared up some. Maybe the phones will be back to working. It'll all be fine."

She nods at me, clearing her throat. "I know." Just like that, every trace of vulnerability is gone.

"Okay, well, let me get some clothes on, and I'll go and see about booking you a room if that's what you still want." I remain still, watching her to see what she'll say. "If you feel safer in here, there are two beds. I don't mind—"

"You're a stranger, Walker. Why the hell would I feel safer with you? I want my own room."

"That's...sort of like a thank you, I guess," I mutter, dropping my phone charger on the bed and turning to walk back to the bathroom.

She's on her feet then. "Why should I say thank you? You're the reason I'm here."

I spin around, pinning her with a glare. "You're right. I *am* the reason you're here, Tibby. The reason you're safe. The reason you're warm and dry. Now, I'm sorry that your plans got ruined, and I'm sorry that your boyfriend or ex or whatever the hell he is sucks, but I'm not the one you're mad at. I haven't done anything wrong here. Okay? So you can stop with the attitude. And maybe..." I trail off, knowing what I was about to say is too cutting, even for the frustration I feel right now.

"Maybe what?" she challenges.

"Maybe next time, pick someone better. Someone who won't leave you stranded in the middle of a snowstorm. Someone who won't hurt you."

Her jaw is set, her eyes stony as she stares at me. "You don't know me, Walker."

"No. I don't. Not for a lack of trying, but I don't. And I don't have to. But you could be a little less..." I search for the word I'm looking for, but I can't find it. "Whatever you're being right now. I'm not the enemy, okay? I'm only trying to help."

"If you want less, go find less, Walker," she says, waving a hand to shoo me away. "I'm not a stray puppy dog. You didn't rescue me."

I raise a brow at her. "Well, I kind of did."

She huffs, shoulders rising, and though I want to hate it, somehow it's adorable. Adorable and completely irritating. "What do you want, dude? A hero's badge? You want me to tell you thank you?"

"We could start with that," I tease. "Look, I'm not expecting you to be grateful, but you could stop acting like I've hurt you or done something wrong by caring."

She pulls her head back, staring at me as if I just started speaking a foreign language. "Do you care?"

I step toward her. Just half a step. Not enough to cause her to release her claws or whatever feral cats do. "Of course, I care. Why else would I be doing this?"

"Why?" Her brows pinch together as she stares at me.

"Why?" I repeat, furrowing my brow. "Why what?"

"Why do you care? You don't know me."

"Because...because you're a human being." I wave my hand at her. "At least in theory."

Her lips pinch together. "In theory?"

"Well, at times you seem more like a robot or feral cat, to be honest."

She folds her arms across her chest, sitting down on the end of the bed with a sigh. "I've always liked cats. They don't trust anyone. I respect that."

I nod. "I'm more of a dog guy."

"Makes sense." When her gaze flicks up toward me, there's a hint of joy there. She's teasing me, I think. "You're basically a golden retriever."

I touch my hair.

"Not because of that. The blond. Well, that helps, I guess. It's the cherry on top. But I'm saying it's everything else about you. You're too happy. Too trusting."

"Fair enough. I'd rather be happy and trusting than bitter and jaded."

She scowls. "Because you've been allowed to be. For women, for me, it's better to be bitter, jaded, and alive than too trusting and dead."

Something cold slides through me, and I instantly miss the shower. The idea of her being dead does something to my emotions I can't rationalize.

"Maybe..."

She looks up at the sound of my voice.

"Maybe you could just be happy and alive."

She chews on the nail of her pointer finger thoughtfully. "I don't think it works like that. Cats and dogs don't typically get along."

"Because cats think dogs are going to hurt them," I point out.

"Sometimes they do. *Usually* they do."

"Maybe so, but not always. Sometimes, cats let their guards down, and they become best friends." I wink.

She rolls her eyes, looking away. "Is that what you want, Walker? To be my *best friend*?"

Warmth blooms in my chest. "I'd settle for not being enemies."

Standing to her feet, she holds out a hand. "Fine. Not enemies, then."

I stare at her hand, at the blood on her sleeve and the wounds on her palms. Whatever happened to her, it was bad.

I reach out, taking her hand in mine. The second our skin connects, lightning shoots through my body, the place where our palms meet is electric and buzzing.

None of this is normal. I'm highly aware of that.

It's the stress of the night and the closeness of our bodies and the way that she's looking at me, and the fact that I haven't been with anyone since I broke up with Alicia a year ago.

It has to be that.

Can only be that.

Realizing I'm still holding her hand and that she hasn't pulled back either, I drop mine away from her. Her eyes land on my bare chest, and the warmth sparks, igniting a full-blown flame inside me. I look away.

"I'll, uh, get some clothes on and then go and see about getting you a room for the night."

Seeming to come out of a trance, she steps away and clears her throat, tucking both hands behind her back. "Great. And...thank you."

I smile at the nicety, touched by the gesture. "No problem."

Once I'm dressed, I exit the bathroom again, my body drenched in sweat from the humidity of the room, fabric sticking to my skin.

She's perched on the edge of the bed, her head resting against the headboard behind her.

"Do you want to come with me?" I ask, gesturing toward the door.

She shakes her head. "I'm going to use the bathroom if that's okay. Freshen up a bit."

"Sure. You can shower if you want. I don't mind."

"I'll wait to have my own bathroom for that, but thanks."

"No problem. When I get back, I'll find you some clean clothes from my bag. I'm sure I have something that will work."

"You don't have to do—"

"I want to." I interrupt her argument. "It's no problem."

"Thanks." She nods, standing up and crossing the room. As she passes me, her hand brushes my arm, and there it is again. The bolt of electricity.

Trying to ignore it, I step out of the motel room and back into the cold. I feel my damp hair turning to ice almost in an instant. The wind whips the snow around, sending it this way and that, making it harder to see anything but this. Hard to imagine there's still a world out there beyond the storm. That just past the darkness and the mess of white, there's a town, then a city, then a world.

I pass through the breezeway, picking up the pace as I near the door to the lobby. When I swing it open, I find another couple standing in front of the desk, deep in conversation. The man is a bit taller than I am, with greasy, slicked-back gray hair, and wearing a denim jacket. The woman is tall, too. Snow clings to every inch of her yellow hair. She offers me a small smile, then looks at the man. The couple stares at me in silence, and I get the feeling I've interrupted an argument. Looking closer, I realize the woman appears on the verge of tears.

The man casts a glance over his shoulder at the desk, then back at me, his eyes narrowing. "You work here?" He runs a hand over his gray mustache.

"Uh, no. I'm just staying here."

"I don't think there's anybody here. Can't get anyone to answer the bell." He taps it several more times in a row to prove his point. "We've been standing here for half an hour, it feels like. You got a phone number to reach the guy?" He points a thumb over his shoulder in the direction Ernest came from earlier.

"I don't, and the phone lines are down. He's not answering the bell?"

The man rings it twice more, then sighs. "Apparently not. Forget it. We'll get 'em later. We've got enough for the night anyway." He gestures for the woman to follow him as he takes a step toward the door.

I move to the side, allowing them past me before I approach the desk.

"Have a nice night," the woman calls back to me. "Stay warm."

The wind catches the door, slamming it shut, and I'm suddenly alone in the silence. Somehow, it's even worse here alone. The quiet of the room, the green-and-yellow-ish glow of the lights overhead, the way they buzz softly. It all has some sort of funhouse effect. Like I've stepped onto the set of a seventies movie and nothing is quite right.

I ring the bell, rapping my knuckles on the top of the desk as I wait. When a few minutes pass, I do it again. This time, twice.

Ching. Ching.

Originally, I assumed the other couple was just impatient, but now I'm realizing they were telling the truth. Ernest doesn't seem to be here. Still, I wait as several more silent minutes pass.

"Ernest?" I call, cupping my hands around my mouth. "You up, bud?" I ring the bell again, then check the time. It's just after midnight, so I wouldn't be surprised if he's sleeping, though I need him to wake up.

I glance down at the desk, which has a stapler, a cup of pens—most of which are missing their caps—and a planner lying on top of it. Nothing else. He already mentioned that room five is empty, so I'm half tempted to place the cash under the keyboard, take the key, and leave a note explaining what happened. I nearly do it, but I'm scared someone would come in and steal the cash, and two hundred-dollar bills are all I have left. My wallet is full of ones and fives, maybe a few tens, but there's not enough to cover the cost of the room, meaning I'd have no way to replace the money if it disappeared.

I guess I could tell him I'll pay him in the morning or he could come to my room to collect, but that feels worse than just leaving it. It feels like stealing somehow.

"Ernest?" I call again, this time louder. "I need that other room."

When he still doesn't answer, I sigh and turn back for the door. Outside, I hurry up the long walkway, noticing lights on in two of the other rooms. When I open the door to mine, the bathroom door is still shut, and I can hear the sound of running water.

I lock the door and cross the room to my bed, opening the suitcase and sorting through the clothes I have in search of something she can wear.

Most of my clothes are casual, but there's a button-down shirt and slacks for church on Sunday. Though I haven't gone in over a year, my parents attend every week, and I know better than to try and skip when I'm staying with them.

I grab a pair of my nicer sweatpants and a plain T-shirt, toying with the idea of loaning her a pair of boxers, but I decide that's a step too far.

I pull out a pair of socks, too, and lay them on top of the pile.

As the water shuts off, the door opens, and she steps out, rubbing her hands together. She stops short when she sees me.

"I didn't hear you get back."

"I just did." I wring my hands together in front of

me. "I've got good news and bad news. Which do you want first?"

"Bad."

Somehow, I expected that. "I can't find Ernest. I rang the bell, called his name a few times, and he didn't come out. Some other couple was in there trying to find him, too."

Her eyes widen. "And? Do you think something's wrong?"

I shake my head. "No. I just think he's sleeping hard and can't hear us calling him. And I don't have any idea where his room is, nor do I want to go snooping to find out."

"Which means?" She glances at the beds warily.

"Which means we're roomies. You'll have your own bed. I swear I won't bother you. If there were any other options, I would take them, but I don't think we have a choice."

I expect her to argue, to tell me a million reasons why this is a terrible idea, but instead, she simply sighs and says, "So what's the good news?"

I pick up the stack of clothes and hand them to her. "I found some clothes you can borrow if you want to take a shower and warm up."

She stares down at them. "They're clean?"

I roll my eyes and put the stack in her hesitant arms. "Yes, you stubborn ass. They're clean."

Ten minutes later, I'm lying in bed, one hand above my head, the other resting on my stomach. I'm so exhausted my entire body hurts. I need to sleep, but I can't. My mind races with more questions as I listen to the steady stream of water in the next room.

What if the roads aren't cleared tomorrow?
What if the storm gets worse and damages the car?
What if the cell towers aren't back up?

We have no way to get food here. The bag of M&M's I bought at the rest area is long gone, and even with Ernie's promise of cereal in the morning, if we have to stay longer than the one night, that's going to become a problem. Not to mention the fact that I've barely managed to contain her tonight, and by tomorrow, there's no telling what she'll attempt in order to escape.

I could hide the keys, I realize, so she won't try to leave. I'm partially scared she's going to wait until I fall asleep and then steal my keys and drive away. But there are only so many places to hide them, and I'm quite certain she'll look in every single one.

I need to clear my head and ease my worries. I need to be out of this space, if only for a few minutes. I slip out of bed and make my way to the door once again, grabbing my coat and slipping it and my boots on.

When this night started, I never dreamed this would be where I ended up. Spending the night with a stranger who makes me feel so conflicted, stranded in the middle of nowhere in a motel without a working television and no cell phone service.

I close the door softly and slip my hands into my pockets, the snow crunching under my feet as I head for the parking lot.

I need to find a snack for my feral cat.

I pass through the parking lot and beyond the two cars, three including ours, that are still there. Ours is back away from the others, which are parked closer to the rooms than the office. My eyes flick to the three lighted windows, and I can't help wondering about the two other people staying here. Are they families, perhaps? People whose holiday travel plans have been interrupted like mine have? Or maybe they're traveling for work or some type of emergency.

A door opens to my right, and I turn my head to see the man and woman from earlier lingering in their doorway. He presses a gentle kiss to her lips, and she leans forward, whispering something in his ear before he turns to face the parking lot.

When he does, his eyes land on me, and I realize I've been awkwardly spying on an intimate moment. Thankfully, rather than make it more awkward by calling me out on it, he lifts his hand in a half wave, then makes his way to the car. I wave back, turning away as he opens the door and leans inside, reaching for something.

I pass the other car, a gray Toyota, slowly, stumbling as my foot slides on a patch of ice hidden underneath the calf-deep snow. I wonder if I could convince Ernest to give us some of the cereal tonight. I know it's meant to be for breakfast, but I can't help thinking Tibby must be hungry. Especially after the traumatic night she had. And while I meant to get her food from the vending machine earlier, her dramatic exit meant she'd missed out on that. I offered her my M&M's, but like I expected, she'd said she wasn't hungry. Honestly, I'm not sure if she declined because she truly wasn't hungry, because her pride wouldn't let her, or because she suspected I'd drugged them.

Either way, finding her something to eat is at the top of my to-do list. There's not much else to do anyway, so why not? A quick snack before bed might be just the thing she needs to finally open up.

The Toyota has a gym sticker on the back of it—one I haven't heard of—and its plates are from out of state, same as mine and the white car.

We're all traveling, and if the fact that the storm has yet to let up is any indication, we might all be here for a few days. I can only hope some of them thought to bring food and supplies, as I suspect what Ernie might have on hand is likely limited.

I push open the door to the lobby and step inside, the warmth of the room washing over me like a wave. I suck in a deep breath, looking around the room for any sign of food.

There is a small table on the far-left side of the room that has a few napkins lying on it and a stack of bowls, but nothing else. I suspect it's where we'll find food in the morning, but it doesn't do any good tonight.

I ring the bell, feeling guilty for doing it. Surely he'll

understand these are special circumstances. If he wants, I'll even pay for it. And I can go ahead and book Tibby her separate room if that's what she'd prefer.

"Ernest?"

He must be a heavy sleeper.

Sleeps like the dead. Chills line my skin as the sentence passes through my mind, and I suddenly can't get out of the lobby quick enough. It's ridiculous, I know. Like running up the stairs toward your bedroom when you've turned off the light on the bottom floor just in case a killer is chasing you. Even still, I can't help it.

I open the door, forgetting about the food for the night, and make my way back to the room. Back inside, I hear the water shutting off as I slip off my coat and drape it over my suitcase. I kick my boots off and place them next to the wall.

Desperate for warmth, I make my way back to the bed and pull the covers down, slipping under them as I yawn.

I listen as she shuffles around in the bathroom, trying my hardest not to think about the fact that she's drying off and dressing just a few feet away from me.

My mind drifts, eyes closing.

I'm zoning out when the door opens, jolting me from what feels like a trance. I rub my eyes as she crosses the room, her dirty clothes tucked under her arm. She places them on the floor and gathers her wet hair in her hands, brushing it over one shoulder, then the next.

I wish I had a hairbrush to let her borrow, but it's not like I have much need for one. I make a mental note to ask Ernest for a spare toothbrush in the morning for her. Once he's had his apparent beauty rest.

"I went for a walk while you were showering."

She quirks a brow. "Yeah?"

"Yeah, to try to get Ernest to wake up, but he didn't. Sorry."

She shrugs one shoulder. "It is what it is."

"Are you hungry?" I sit up in bed as she makes her way back toward the bathroom.

She stops and turns around. "Why? Do you have food?"

"No." I look down at my hands. "I thought you might be, so I was also going to ask Ernest for cereal, but I couldn't wake him up. If you're hungry, though, I could try again." I don't know why I'm offering. I desperately don't want to try again, but I also feel like I would do anything to make sure she's comfortable and safe. The protective feelings I have about her aren't natural. I'm starting to think exhaustion is getting the best of me.

"I'm fine, Walker." She sighs, disappearing into the bathroom and reappearing a few minutes later. "But thank you." She avoids my eyes as she heads for the bed, pulling back the covers and adjusting the pillows. Just then, my eyes fall to her legs, at the red patch blooming on the gray of my sweatpants.

"Are you okay?" I shoot up in bed, eyes bugging.

"What?" She spins around to look at me. "I'm fine. What do you mean?"

"You're bleeding." I point to the blood on the fabric covering her shin.

She pales, looking down in horror but not confusion. When she bends down, she pulls her pant leg up slightly, revealing a deep gash along her shin bone.

"I'm so sorry," she says, shaking her head.

"Sorry?" I'm out of bed then, bending down next to her. "What are you sorry for?"

"For bleeding on your clothes. I didn't mean to—"

I put a finger under her chin, lifting her face so she'll look at me. My eyes lock with hers—dark brown with hints of gold—and I hear, rather than see, her take a breath.

"I don't care about the pants," I tell her, keeping my voice low, my lips hardly moving. Everything suddenly feels hazy. "I care about you. Are *you* okay?"

She swallows, blinking, and looks back down at her leg. "I, um, I fell earlier. On the pavement. When Craig and I were fighting. I hit a rock." She stands, starting to head for the bathroom, but I beat her to it.

"I've got it." I return a few moments later with a fresh roll of toilet paper and begin tearing off pieces, handing them to her. "It's not exactly medical-grade bandaging, but it'll help."

"Thanks." She presses the tissue to her wound. "I thought it had stopped bleeding, but the warm water from the shower must've made it start again."

I want to ask if she needs to go to the hospital, but really, what good would it do? I couldn't get her there unless I called an ambulance, which I can't do until the phones are back up. And even if, by some miracle, the phones were to start working again, truth be told, I'm not sure they'd make it here in this storm anyway.

"It might need stitches," I tell her gently, bending down and lifting the tissue for a second so I can get a better look. It's relatively deep and about as long as my pinkie finger. "You said you fell?"

"Yes." She looks away as I lift her leg to get a better look.

"You were fighting?"

She nods and clears her throat. "It wasn't a big deal."

"Is that what happened to your hands?" I gesture to the wounds across her palms.

She studies them, looking unbothered. "Yeah, I scraped them. They're fine."

I put the tissue back over the wound on her shin. "You should keep pressure on it. I'll be right back." I cross the room again and grab a towel from the bathroom, returning to tie it around her leg gently. "This will help hold the tissue in place so you don't have to worry about it through the night. Hopefully tomorrow we can get you some real bandages. I wish you'd said something earlier. Maybe we could've found something at the rest area when we were there. The cut needs to be cleaned out with peroxide at the very least. The scrapes on your hands too."

"Yeah, I know. I didn't think about it then. It wasn't bleeding at that point, and I was a bit preoccupied with being kidnapped."

I scowl. "Try rescued."

"Rescue usually requires a willingness to go." The words would sting if I didn't sense the playfulness of her tone.

"No one shoved you in the car, last I checked. Just a bit of healthy persuasion." I nudge her shoulder with my finger. If I hadn't stopped tonight, I wouldn't know this woman, and that feels impossible. And in just a few days, hours maybe, she'll be long gone. Just a distant memory. It doesn't seem fair.

"That's not how I remember it."

"Seems like the cold got to your head."

To my surprise, she smirks, and her eyes linger on mine for several seconds. There's something so mysterious about her, so confident and distant, it just makes me want to know more. To ask more. She looks away abruptly, turning her face to look at her leg again, ending whatever the hell just happened between us.

"*Anyway*, I thought I was fine." She pulls the towel tighter around her leg than I'd had it. "Thank you, though."

"Sure." I move to stand but stop at eye level with her, staring into her wild and somehow fearful yet bold eyes again. The woman is a walking contradiction. "Can I ask you something?"

Lips parted, she nods. "Mm-hmm."

I clear my throat, running a hand over my face as the sobering question fills my head. "Did he—*does* he—hurt you a lot?"

She blinks, clearly not expecting that to be the question I asked. "Craig?"

"Yeah."

"He wasn't abusive, if that's what you mean, no. He was—*is*—just...I don't know. He's just hard to get along with sometimes. Stubborn and hot-tempered." She lowers the leg of her sweatpants and drops her foot to the ground. "He didn't care enough to fight with me. He was too caught up in himself."

I wait for her to say more, but when she doesn't, I press her. "What do you mean?"

"He was just sort of checked out, I guess. His job was...really demanding. Physically and emotionally, and he just didn't care about me. Not really. And I don't say that for pity. I'm over it. It's just the truth. He spent more time at the gym than he ever did with me."

The truth of her words sits heavy in my chest. I hate him. I want to kill him for ever making her feel so unloved and unwanted.

"He didn't do this if that's what you're thinking," she adds. "My leg, I mean. Honestly, it was my fault. And not in a 'it was my fault because I made him mad' sort of way. We were arguing and—or, well, *I* was arguing, and he was mostly ignoring me—and I'd had enough, so I got out of the car and tried to run away. But it was snowing and slick, and I slipped on a stupid patch of ice. I went down hard, and my leg hit a rock or a piece of asphalt or something, sliced it open. My hands got all scraped up from the fall. It hurt, of course, and it was made worse by the cold, but I..." She looks away with a solemn expression. "He didn't come to check on me. He just drove away."

"And I found you after?"

She nods. "Yeah. I'd been walking for an hour, maybe, when you found me. I was so distracted I didn't realize how far I'd walked. My phone was still in the car because I never thought he'd actually leave—" She cuts herself off as her voice cracks. "Anyway, that was that. He's not abusive, he's just an asshole."

"Well, good. I'm glad. You don't deserve to be hurt."

"No one does," she says, lifting the covers up and slipping into bed.

"So, what do you like to do for fun?" I sit on the edge of my bed, watching her.

Her head tilts to the side. "What?"

"You know, *fun*. Enjoyment. The thing most people experience now and again."

It's her turn to scowl at me then, and she purses her lips for good measure. "Yes, Walker. I'm aware of what *fun* is. I just don't know why you're asking."

"I just thought we could get to know each other a little bit. Since we're stuck together for a while."

She shakes her head. "In just a few hours, we'll be on

the road again." There's a confidence in her voice I don't expect. She's certain we'll be leaving soon, while I don't see how we could. Stubborn as she is, I'm worried she'll find a way. "You won't be stuck with me much longer."

"There are worse people to be stuck with." I run my feet along the stiff carpet. "You're not the *worst* company."

"I'd hate to meet the worst, then," she says softly. When I look up, she's twirling a piece of hair around her finger, seemingly lost in thought.

"It'd definitely be Ernest," I quip. "I mean, that guy can clearly sleep through a tornado."

"Or a blizzard," she adds with a laugh. Our eyes meet again, and there's that moment, that electric moment, where something charges inside of me, like a balloon being blown up or pressing your tongue to a battery. I don't know how to explain it, and I'm not sure I've ever felt it before.

Ending the moment, she looks away.

"Seriously, Tibby. I know it's been a shitty night for you, but I'm glad you're here. I'm...I'm really glad I found you."

She meets my eyes again, hers bouncing back and forth between mine as she makes me wait to hear her response. Eventually, she opens her mouth and reaches for the lamp. "We should get some sleep. Good night, Walker."

I sit in stunned silence and darkness for what feels

like an eternity. Finally, I sigh, the balloon in my chest deflating in an instant.

"Good night." I slip into bed, bathed in darkness, hoping she'll say something else. Anything else.

But she doesn't. The only sounds in the room are those of pattering of the snow and ice on the windows and the wind howling as the storm rages outside.

CHAPTER NINE

BEFORE

I've changed my mind again. I was wrong earlier. I just hadn't given myself enough time to process everything.

My final verdict is that everyone should commit murder on snow if they want to get away with it. At least, if you have enough privacy and time to wait for it to melt.

With the snow spread around, the evidence of my crime tossed here and there, I'm feeling good as I walk away. It's how I always feel after a night like this, after ending a life, settling a score, but this time is different.

Special.

His body is gone. I heard the animals doing the dirty work for me. This time I know, when the storm is just a distant memory and the weather warms up enough to melt the snow away, every trace of what I've done will be gone. As much a part of the earth as his body is now.

Aside from his bones, which will no doubt be torn

apart and scattered throughout the woods long before anyone enters them, there will be nothing left to tie us together, to hint that there was a crime at all. His blood will soak into the mud, the dirt, the soil, and anything left of his body will nourish the plants and the animals. It'll be the one selfless thing he's ever done.

When I gave up on digging the grave, I threw my shovel in a ravine nearby. The icy water is still rushing so fast, moving it along so quickly, it'll never be traced back to this area if it's found at all.

Someone will just think it's been lost or misplaced. They may keep it and use it to plant the vegetables they feed their children with, even. Consider it my good deed. A donation.

I cross the woods slowly, studying the car where it sits. It's stalled along the side of the road, but so far no one has gotten out. The headlights shine, illuminating the empty road ahead. In front of it, snow falls in every direction, with thick, heavy snowflakes that I know are already doing the work of covering the crime scene I just left.

I need a car.

I need this person's car.

The thought is firm in my mind at this point. Whoever is in this car will have to go. It's a twist of fate, a choice they made to stop, and now I have to kill them.

When you need things, the universe has a way of putting them directly in your path. Now, standing just feet away from the car at the edge of the treeline, that's never felt more poignant than at this exact moment.

Quickly, before they can drive away, I formulate a plan. Once I have it, I barrel out of the tree line, running forward with my hands over my head and waving them frantically.

No one has rolled down a window or stepped out by the time I reach the car, and as I get closer, I can see the two figures inside. They're illuminated by the glow of the radio in the dashboard. Teenagers, from the looks of it. She's in his lap on the driver's side, her shirt removed, breasts exposed. Their kisses are the passionate kind that belongs exclusively to young lovers, the kind of kisses that make the world around them disappear entirely.

The kind of kisses that keep them blind to the stranger, the murderer, standing just outside their car.

I bang on the window, needing to draw their attention. To get them out of the car where this will be easier. Less messy.

The girl screams and falls out of his lap, covering herself with her hands.

"What the fuck?" His voice is so loud I can hear him outside the car.

"Drive!" She points ahead with one hand, using the other to grab her shirt from the back floorboard. "Please, drive, Ben."

"It's fine." He cracks the window, easing his seat up. "Yeah? Can we help you?" He's adjusting himself in his seat, out of breath and clearly frustrated.

"Help." I force myself to pant. To seem out of breath. To cry and whine and beg and seem as helpless and harmless as I can. "There's a dog that fell into the ravine. I keep trying to get it to come to me, but it's hurt and scared. I need your help to get it before it drowns."

In the seat next to him, the girl has pulled the shirt back over her head to cover herself and is staring at me with a worried expression.

"A dog?" She glances at the boy, and I can tell she doesn't believe me. Doesn't feel safe. I'm not worried, though. I can already tell he's the only one I have to convince.

"Where did you come from?" The boy looks around, appearing nervous, though I suspect he's more worried about what I saw than that I might be a danger to them.

"I was just passing through. You probably saw my car a few miles back." They exchange a look that tells me they did. "I was driving, heading home for the holidays, and the dog just darted out in front of me. I almost couldn't stop in time, nearly hit it." I run a hand over my mouth. "It's too cold for any animal to be out in this, so I pulled over to try to get it in the car and check for a collar to get it home, but it took off. I'm just trying to get it somewhere warm before the storm gets worse. And I left my phone in the car. Please. Come on. We're wasting time. I need your help before it drowns or floats down the creek too far and we can't get to it. It's lucky I saw your headlights. No one else has driven by and I don't think I can save him on my own at this point."

They exchange worried glances, but eventually, the boy nods and pushes the door open. "Okay. Yeah, I'll help. You wait here," he tells her, ever the gentleman.

"I'm not staying here alone." She's out of the car in an instant, hurrying down into the woods with us.

"You kids really shouldn't be parked on the interstate like that," I say. "It's not safe. Especially with the storm tonight. Someone loses control, they'll skid right into you."

The boy runs a hand through his hair, fluffing it like teenagers do. "Yeah, sorry." He takes her hand, pulling her close to him.

"Where's the dog?" the girl asks when we've been walking a while. "How far away is it?"

"Just right up here." I hear the sounds of the creek as we grow closer to it. "It was down in the water but trying to climb out. I think I saw a shallow spot where we can climb down and call it to us. Between the three of us, we should be able to get him out of the water safely. I just didn't want to chance it alone."

We reach the edge of the water, staring down at the creek several feet below us.

"Where is it?" he shouts over the rushing water.

"I don't know..." I search the water, looking for this imaginary dog with all my might. "Oh, I hope it didn't get carried away. Check down there!" I shout, pointing forward toward the water up ahead. Both of them rush forward at my command, trying to find this animal, which gives me the perfect opportunity.

I pull the knife out, shoving it forward and into the boy's lower back.

"Ah!" He jerks, cries out, and turns to look at me. "What did you do?" He tries to reach for the knife, swiping a hand toward it as I pull it out. I stab him twice more until his knees give out. At the same time, the girl notices what's happened and begins to scream.

Rather than trying to help him, save him, or do anything heroic, she does the predictable thing and runs.

I'm very aware of the fact that I could've gone about this a different way. I could've threatened them. Or just lured them from the car and taken it. But either option would be too risky once they'd seen my face. I can't leave anything up to chance, and God knows how teenagers like to run their mouths.

Without an ounce of regret, I grab hold of the boy's shirt, taking the keys from his pants pocket. He doesn't fight me, doesn't struggle. He's limp in my arms as I toss him into the ravine below us. It's quick. He goes over fast, lands face down in the creek, and disappears. He was dead before he hit the water.

I go after the girl next. She's still screaming, and that has to stop.

There should be no one around for miles, but on the off chance there is, I can't let them hear her. I lunge forward, grabbing her head and pulling her down on top of me as we both fall to the ground. I cover her mouth with my hand.

A new way of killing someone for me, but why not? Let's give it a whirl.

I apply more pressure as she struggles, wrapping my legs around her body to keep her as still as possible. She writhes under my grasp, pushing and pulling air from her lungs with every bit of her strength. Her legs and arms flail as she reaches for me, punching the space between us with all her might. Her hands reach out, slapping at the air, but it's no use. She's a fighter, I'll give her that.

But so am I.

I squeeze harder, refusing to let go until she goes still in my arms. Slowly, I lift one finger at a time. When I'm sure she's really gone, I stand, dusting the snow from my clothes as I stare down at her limp body.

In the water, the boy's body has floated to the surface, face down, moving with the current. I grab hold of her—one hand on the back of her shirt, the other on the waist of her jeans—and drag her to the edge.

She's thin. Easy to move. Probably skipped meals, definitely skipped dessert, to look this way. To be perfect, even in death.

With two easy pushes, she goes over the cliff and into the water below. I dust my hands and clean the knife off in the snow. Problem solved.

Just like that, I have a car.

CHAPTER TEN

TIBBY

I don't know how I managed to fall asleep in a room with this stranger, but somehow I did. I use the word *sleep* lightly. I slept, though not well. I tossed and turned, uncovered and covered, struggling to find a way to be comfortable. When I'm fully awake again, I realize the struggle was likely more internal than external.

I survey the room slowly. It's still dark out, and the clock on the nightstand tells me it's just minutes after two in the morning.

I check Walker's bed from where I'm lying and notice it's empty. Instantly, I sit up, taking in my surroundings from the new angle. The bathroom door stands open, light off.

"Walker?" I call, my heart picking up speed as I realize I'm alone in the dark without a clue where he is.

I stand from the bed, jumping far away from the edge so a monster doesn't get my feet. As a fully grown adult, I still reserve the right to do that, *thank you very much*, especially after the night I've had.

I peek out the window, staring into the dark parking lot, and breathe out a sigh of relief.

His car is still there. He hasn't left me. I don't know why I feel so much comfort over that realization, but I know that I hate it.

I hate myself for trusting him, for wanting to stay with him, for telling him anything about me, and for falling asleep.

I've gotten weak. Careless. Trusting.

I move around to the nightstand and flip on the lamp, placing my leg on the bed to check my wound. The towel Walker wrapped around my calf fell off in my sleep and there are just a few pieces of toilet tissue still stuck to it, but it seems to have stopped bleeding, though there is dried blood all across my shin. I pull the tissues off and toss them into the trash before slipping on my boots and stepping outside.

I need to find him, to make sure we're okay. That everything's okay.

My breath freezes in the air in front of me, forming a white puff of fog. The snow has finally stopped, at least for now, and the world around me is silent.

"He went that way," a man's voice says from my left. I jump at the sound, turning to face it. The man standing there looks to be in his fifties or sixties, with thin, graying hair slicked back over his head and a silver mustache.

"Huh?"

"You looking for the manager? He just went that way."

"Oh." My heart plummets. "No, I wasn't, but thanks."

He shrugs, puffing on the cigarette between his lips before pulling it away and flicking the ash. "Figured your room is probably as shitty as ours. Heat barely works. No TV. I just got him to come fix some things, so you can catch him if you need anything. Before he goes back to bed," he scoffs, rolling his eyes.

"I'm okay. Did you... Did you see another man by any chance?"

He squints, staring into space. "I can't say that I did."

"Okay, thanks." I cross the parking lot, the snow crunching underfoot as I make my way toward the lobby. I need to find him, though I hate feeling that way.

After tonight, after everything happened with Craig, I swore to myself I'd never rely on a man again. Never allow myself to need a man or even want a man in the way I once needed and wanted him.

Needing someone, caring about someone, trusting someone...it makes you weak. He made me weak.

And now Walker is doing the same thing.

Then again, he doesn't look at me the way Craig did. Craig never took care of me like Walker has tonight, not even in the beginning. He was carefree and fun above all else. Never one for anything serious. The life of the party. A protector, maybe, but never a caretaker.

He'd fight someone over me but never fight for me, if that makes sense. For Craig, it was all about possession. Walker doesn't feel that way.

It's strange, and honestly, it's probably just the storm, hunger, and exhaustion driving me crazy, but I swear I feel connected to him in a way I never have.

Like he was meant to find me tonight.

Yeah, definitely the exhaustion.

Still, I want to find him.

Where could he be? Maybe he got hungry and decided to go try to find something to eat again, but Ernest said any food other than what he has for breakfast is pretty far away. Maybe he just needed to get some fresh air to clear his head or try to find a signal to call his family. I try to remember if his phone was still on the nightstand where he'd had it charging, but I'm not sure.

Maybe he's gone to get a weapon so he can kill me.

I force the thought away as I study my surroundings, searching for him in the snow. The brightness of it in contrast to the darkness of the world around us is giving me a headache.

Maybe he left me.

My stomach goes hollow, almost as if it's caving in on itself as I glance across the parking lot. His car is still here. He didn't leave.

He wouldn't.

I shouldn't trust him this much.

I *don't* trust him this much.

Looking away from the car, I check to see if the man is still there next to his room watching me. When I discover he is, I turn away quickly, then head for the lobby. Maybe Ernest has seen him or can point me in the right direction.

Walker, where are you?

I push open the lobby door and step inside the quiet room, surprised to find it empty. The buzzing from the lights overhead instantly amplifies my headache.

"Ernest?" I call, keeping my voice low. "Walker?" Everything in this silent space feels like shouting. I lean forward over the desk, like I might find him crouching there ready to jump out and surprise me.

Though I don't see him, something else does catch my eye.

Something dark red, nearly black.

My body goes instantly cold as I struggle to make sense of what I'm looking at.

That can't be what I think it is. It's impossible. Isn't it?

I glance up, staring around the room and hoping someone will come out. That Ernest will appear from around the corner with a rag and cleaner and say he just spilled some barbecue sauce and was in the process of cleaning it up.

"Ernest? Ernest's wife? Walker? Is anyone there?" I ring the bell, waiting and listening. My heart picks up speed in my chest, racing as I stand there in total and complete silence.

Finally done waiting, I walk around the desk against

my better judgment, bending down behind it with trembling hands as I take in what I'm seeing. A small, red puddle of what looks like smeared blood covers the floor, with splatters along the wood of the backside of the desk.

I cover my mouth, trying to catch my breath.

No.

No.

No.

No.

No.

It can't be this. It has to be something else. It has to be...Jell-O. Ketchup. Jam. Literally anything else. But it isn't.

It just isn't.

I swallow, following the thin trail of blood with my eyes to where it leads. Behind the desk, there's just a small amount of space and a wall with a single metal door. The trail of blood goes directly to it.

I don't want to open the door. I shouldn't open it.

Whatever I find in there will only make everything worse. I should go look for Walker. Or the other people staying here. Ask them to help me. Ask them to call the police.

But that's not an option. It can't be.

I hate asking for help. Refuse to do it. I'm a strong, capable, independent woman, and I can open creepy closets all on my own, *thank you*.

I step toward the door in a sort of half-aware state.

None of this makes sense. Maybe I'm still dreaming. Maybe I never actually woke up. That's possible, isn't it?

Sure it is. It's likely, even. More likely than this. I could still be safe in my bed. It could be that none of this is happening. It's probably not happening, in fact.

I mean, what are the odds that any of this could be real? No, it has to be a dream. I fell asleep thinking about my bloody shin, and now I'm dreaming about seeing blood where it quite literally cannot be.

Wake up, Tibby.

Wake up.

But even as I try to convince myself I'm wrong or delusional or dreaming, I know I'm not. I know from the chill on my skin, the odd buzzing in my ears, and the yellowish glow...*I know* that this is real. That it's happening and that I'll never be the same.

Briefly, as I reach out to open the door, I consider walking away. Pretending none of this happened, that I never saw the blood. Going back to bed and letting this be someone else's problem. But I can't.

So I open the door.

Only, it's not a closet at all. Cold air hits me in an instant, and I'm staring into an open lot behind the motel. The blood trail stops a few feet into the snow, and I feel relief. Maybe someone had a nosebleed—or several —and they fixed it. There are no bodies here. No proof anyone is hurt. Maybe it truly is something that got spilled.

I'm so tired, and the lights are so weird in there, it's not impossible, I suppose.

I step out into the snow, looking around, but see no one. I'm about to go back inside when I hear something to my left. From just around the corner of the building.

Someone is over there.

CHAPTER ELEVEN

WALKER

I still can't sleep, despite how tired I am. I feel this nervous energy inside of me. Jittery. Like I can't sit still. I can't stop moving. Adrenaline from everything that's happened tonight perhaps, but I need it to go away.

I need to breathe easier, but I have no idea how. There's too much to stress over, too much than can and has gone wrong.

As the motel comes back into view, I pull my hands from my pockets and check my phone again.

Still no service.

This storm has to be one of the worst ones I've seen in my life. I remember an ice storm in 2009 when I was in high school that knocked out the power in our town for nearly two weeks, cell service too. The whole town ran on generators, and the government sent in freeze-dried military food for us to eat. At the time, it felt like an adventure. I remember spending nights in our living room in front of the fireplace with blankets covering the doorway to keep the heat in. I remember turning on the generator long enough for one person to shower. As a kid, all that shit feels like an adventure, I guess. You have no real responsibility. It's all just fun. Maybe a little inconvenient when you can't charge your phone and talk to your girlfriend, but other than that, it wasn't a big deal.

Now, it feels major. Now, I understand the repercussions. I'm hoping we'll be able to get a tow truck out here to get us to town in the morning. If we wake up tomorrow and the roads still aren't open, I'm going to have to find a way to get Tibby something to eat. We have the cereal and milk Ernest mentioned, if the other guests don't eat it all first, but it's not much. And he'll need it for himself and his wife, too. Especially if things are bad for too long.

Tough times change people in the worst ways.

We have water and coffee in the room, at least, but I'm kicking myself over not grabbing food at the last gas station I stopped at before I found her. If I'd had the foresight to grab a bag of chips or a sandwich—something other than that bag of M&M's at the rest stop—at least we'd have something small to get us through.

Now, in just a few hours, the sun will be coming up, and with cell towers still down, I don't have much hope the roads are cleared or even safer to drive on than they were when we arrived.

I stop at my car and check the back seat, hoping I

might've forgotten about a bag of something to snack on, but there's nothing.

I yawn as I close the door, knowing I should go back to the room and try to get some sleep, but I can't. Not with her sleeping next to me. Not while the world is falling apart and my simple plans for this holiday weekend are unraveling at the seams.

Tomorrow is New Year's Eve—today, actually, I guess —and here I am, stranded in the middle of nowhere with a woman who seems to actively hate me.

I'm pacing around the parking lot when I hear someone moving closer to me. I spin around, not sure what to expect, and my eyes land on a terrified-looking Tibby.

"What are you doing?" I ask.

At the same time, she blurts out, "Where were you?"

"I went for a walk to clear my head," I tell her, trying to understand the strange expression on her face. "Tibby? What's wrong?"

She shakes her head, running her trembling fingers over her bottom lip with this sort of faraway expression on her face. "I, um, I... Well, I think something happened. Something's wrong."

My body goes even colder, though I don't know how it's possible, as a lump forms in my throat. "What do you mean?"

"There's..." She pauses, rubbing her lips together. "I think there's blood, um, in the...in the lobby."

Every muscle in my body seems to tense up. "What?"

Her eyes meet mine finally, so full of fear and uncertainty that it's painful. "Did you see it when you were in there earlier?"

"No. Of course not. I mean, I don't think so. I'm sure it's not blood," I tell her, not sure of anything at all.

"There's a trail. It...it leads to the door, but then it just stops. I don't understand what's happening here, Walker, but I have a bad feeling. We need to go."

Something clicks in my head, and I stare at her, trying to keep my tone from being judgmental. "Are you just saying this because you're trying to get us to leave? I just walked down the road trying to get service, and everything's still covered. The roads are trash right now, Tibby. I swear. It's not safe—"

"That's not why I'm doing this," she says quickly, her voice echoing in the quiet night.

I shuffle in place, the snow crunching underfoot.

"I know what I saw. It's blood. Will you just come look, and then you'll see? Please?"

I sigh, puffing out a breath of visible air. "Yeah, okay."

She takes my hand, and my entire body lights up, no longer cold in any sense of the word. I let her lead me around the building and up the walk to the lobby. She pushes the door open, and we step inside. The warmth of the room envelops me, and I have to wonder why I ever left the heat in the first place.

Wasting no time, she leads me around the desk. "Come on. It's over here." She stops behind the desk, pointing to a small puddle of a thick, nearly black substance. "I came looking for you and couldn't find you. And then I rang the bell and called for Ernest, but no one came. I'm not sure what's going on, but..."

I bend down next to the puddle, studying it for any signs that it could be something other than blood, but I know I won't find it. She's right.

It *is* blood.

My stomach clenches, and it feels as if I'm a rubber band waiting to snap. Everything is falling apart, and this is just another domino that's been knocked over. Another thing that has gone wrong.

"We have to leave, Walker." She brushes her hand over my shoulder. "Please. We have to leave now."

But we can't.

CHAPTER TWELVE

BEFORE

For a teenager's car, this thing isn't bad. He kept it clean, I'll give him that. Aside from two cups from a fast-food restaurant in the cup holders, there's not a bit of trash in here. A thick coat sits in the back seat that might be useful later.

I'll drive this car a few miles, dump it at a gas station or rest area, and find a new one. I can't be in it for long. I didn't hide the bodies well enough. Eventually, someone will find them, though with any luck it won't be tonight.

It's starting to snow again. I fiddle with the car's knobs, switching it to the radio rather than its previous Bluetooth connection, and search for a station that will come in clearly.

This storm has knocked nearly everything out, and it seems to be getting worse by the minute. As if to confirm my thoughts, the second I land on a radio station, I hear a man's voice.

"Well, folks, it's going to be a rough night here in the Heartland. The winter storm moving through the area has taken a turn for the worse, altering some of the predictions from earlier this evening when we told you it looked as though things would ease up as the storm system moved farther south. As of right now, it looks as if the worst is yet to come. We're looking at another eight to ten inches of snow by morning for most of the area, and the farthest counties south could be hit with an additional one to two inches of sleet and ice. Of course, things could change, and we'll keep you posted on what to expect as we monitor the storm system, but please, folks, if you don't have to be on the roads tonight, don't. Stay home, warm, and safe, and allow the highway teams to do their jobs and get these roads cleared just as quickly and safely as they can. We're looking for temperatures to warm up by the end of the week, so an end is in sight. We're just going to have to be patient. As for traffic conditions—"

I switch the radio off, slamming my hand into the steering wheel and cursing. The storm getting worse, lasting longer, just means my time is limited. The car's low-fuel light is on, so the first exit I see with a gas station, I pull off and fill it up. Paying with cash, of course. I keep my head low, my hood pulled up.

In a storm like this, no one would think to question it. I'm simply your average, freezing-cold traveler trying to warm up. Not someone who just murdered three people and is now trying to hide their face.

The more I think about it, the more convinced I am that snowstorms make the perfect setting for murder. Maybe I'll move to Alaska after this.

Before I leave, I use the restroom and get a coffee to keep me awake. I consider getting a snack but decide against it, though I do pick up a copy of the local paper on a whim.

Quiet town. The front page is simply an article about the Christmas parade from last week.

I smile to myself, thinking the paper will be much more interesting this week. Perhaps it could compete with the cities around here—Marion, Carbondale, or Belleville potentially, though I don't think any of these tiny cities see much action either.

That'll all change with my passing through town.

Consider it a public service.

People love drama.

CHAPTER THIRTEEN

TIBBY

"We have to leave now," I repeat when he doesn't say anything. "*Now*, now. I don't care about the roads. Something weird is going on here, and I don't want to stay. I don't feel safe here."

"I'm sure it's nothing," he says, his voice dry and powerless. "We should find Ernest. See if he can help us figure out what's going on."

"You said you couldn't find him earlier when you tried to book me a separate room." I narrow my gaze at him. "And I couldn't find him now. He didn't come when I rang the bell or called for him."

"You're right. What if something happened to him?" He reaches across the desk and rings the bell several times, eyes darting back and forth with his obviously racing thoughts.

"There was a man who said he saw him," I remember aloud. "He said he was coming in here. That's how I found the blood. I was... I was looking for you." I hate admitting that to him and can't help wondering what he'll read into it. "I just wanted to see if you'd found him or something when I realized you weren't in the room. I was hoping you'd found a way for me to get my own so we didn't have to stay together."

It doesn't seem like he's listening. "What man? Someone saw Ernest? When was this?"

"I don't know, maybe twenty minutes ago. There was a man outside one of the rooms. He had gray, greasy hair and a mustache. He was smoking a cigarette. I'm guessing he's staying here. He said he saw Ernest—well, he called him *the manager*, not by his actual name, but he had to have meant Ernest, right? Anyway, he said he saw him coming this way."

"Good," he says with a puff of air. "Good. That's good. That means he was okay then. Twenty minutes ago. We should go look for him, though. We need to find him and make sure he's still okay." He rings the bell again and cups his hands around his mouth. "Ernest? Ernie? You in here, man?" When several minutes pass, and Ernest still doesn't answer, Walker takes off in the direction he came from when we first checked in.

Down the hall, heading in a direction neither of us know, he leads me to a set of three doors. He pauses, checking to make sure I'm with him, then knocks on the first door.

"Ernest? Um, you...you in there?"

A lump sits firmly in my throat, refusing to go away.

My heart pounds in my ears as we wait, but we get no answer. He twists the knob, and we look inside the dimly lit room. It's an open living space, with a kitchen on the end of the room closest to us and a living room on the other. In the living room section, there are two matching recliners in front of a television, which is turned on to the local news. At least *his* TV works, I guess.

Walker flips on the light so we get a better view of the space, but it's small and ordinary. The kitchen counter is littered with tiny orange bottles, evidence of his wife's illness. The sink has a few dishes in it, and there's a box from a frozen dinner lying on the counter next to the microwave. In the living room, there's a single end table with an ashtray and a half-filled bottle of Dr Pepper in between the recliners. On the floor, there is a pair of black socks and another bottle of Dr Pepper, this one empty.

Walker crosses the room, checking for any sign of the man, and stops short when he reaches the recliners, staring down at something I can't see.

"Is he there?" I whisper, hoping we've found Ernest asleep in his chair and this is all somehow just a misunderstanding.

He shakes his head, putting a finger to his lips. I cross the small room quickly and stare down at an elderly woman sitting in the chair. She's so tiny she almost looks fake. She can't weigh more than ninety pounds, and her thin skin is a sickly gray color. For just a moment, I worry she's dead, but when I see her chest rising and falling with soft breaths, I'm relieved to be wrong. Her hair has been combed neatly, the gray tendrils cascading over her bony shoulders. Someone—Ernest, I'm assuming—has wrapped her lower half in a blanket and she has one fuzzy-socked foot sticking out. Carefully, Walker moves the blanket to cover the foot. Despite being very sick, or perhaps because of it, this woman is obviously incredibly loved and cared for.

Thinking of Ernest there with her alone in this sleepy little town makes me feel sad but also nostalgic in a way. Like I'm missing something I've never had, something I will probably never have. What Ernest and his wife have is special. It's the dream. To have someone who will care for you even when the worst happens.

It makes me think of Craig, who would never be that man. I'm not sure how I was ever so blinded by him. He was always the man who stayed away when I was sick so he wouldn't catch it and forgot the things I'd told him more often than not.

"We should go." Chills line my skin over the thought of being caught. "He could be back any second."

Just then, something on the news catches my eye, and I look over. Walker is headed toward me, but I hold up a hand to stop him and point at the television.

"Look."

He turns as I say the word. The television's volume is down so low it's hard to hear, but I get all I need to know from the headline showing along the bottom.

There's a split screen image of two teenagers' faces. A

boy and a girl. Young, beautiful, full of joy and hope. Their full lives should be ahead of them. Clearly loved.

But the breaking news headline reads: **Two Teens Reported Missing, Last Believed to be Traveling Along I-57 Toward Chicago.**

CHAPTER FOURTEEN

WALKER

Tibby rushes across the room, turning the volume up on the television just in time to hear the news anchor saying, "Police have asked the public to be on the lookout for a pair of teens tonight as the storm throughout the area worsens. Ben Harris and Nicole Truby, both just nineteen years old, are believed to be traveling north along I-57 toward Chicago. The teens' families last spoke to them before the storm set in and they have been unable to contact the couple for the past several hours. At this time, police have no reason to believe the teens are in any danger as road conditions and several road closures have made a significant impact on travel times, along with cell towers being out all across the region, but as a precaution, if anyone has any information about the couple's whereabouts, police are asking that you please contact—"

She flips the television off. "That's this area." Her eyes are wild and filled with fear as she crosses the room.

"What if they were here? What if they were one of the other people staying here, and this is their blood and—"

"Tibby, breathe. It just said they were traveling *near* here," I point out, jogging to keep up with her. "We have no reason to even suspect that they're dead or hurt or that there's anything wrong. Cell towers are down everywhere. They're probably just caught out in this like everyone else with no service. It didn't mention the motel. You have no reason to think that blood in the lobby had anything to do with those kids. Or that it means anything at all. I'm sure they're fine."

She doesn't slow down, though—ever stubborn, and now terrified as she exits the room and dashes down the hall, then into the lobby. She spins around, pinning me with a glare. "You're telling me it's all just a coincidence? We find blood and then find out that there are people— *kids*—missing in this area. How many people are realistically traveling the interstate in this storm?"

I huff out a breath. "I'm telling you there's no need to assume there's a connection unless they tell us otherwise. It didn't even say they're definitely missing. She just said their families couldn't reach them. It sounds like they're just trying to make sure they're safe in the storm. We didn't pass any broken-down cars or anything. I'm sure they're fine."

She turns away from me again, rolling her eyes, and pulls open the door, stepping out into the icy night. "They would've had to stop here. If they were traveling on fifty-seven, they would've had to stop when the road closed. That would've taken them right this way."

As she picks up speed, I work to keep pace with her, just waiting for one of us to trip on a hidden patch of ice in the parking lot. "They could've been hours ahead of us. They might've made it through. You're panicking over nothing. You just need to calm down. Look—"

"Don't tell me to calm down!" she shouts, stopping once again and wagging a finger at me. "We need to leave, Walker. It may not be related, but something is wrong here. Ernest is missing, and—"

"*Missing?* Come on. That's a bit of a stretch, don't you think?" I gesture back toward the lobby. "We didn't check the other rooms in the hall. For all you know, he's safe and sound asleep in his bed."

"And he just left his wife in her recliner?"

"Okay. Maybe he was in the bathroom."

"And he's been missing all night? Come on, Walker. Make that make sense. Even if he's not hurt, then someone else is. Someone's blood is all over that lobby, and something bad is happening here. I just know it."

I inhale, sensing how serious her panic is. I get it, honestly. Something about all of this feels wrong, but leaving right now is impossible. Still, I can see in her expression she isn't going to let me argue that point.

I drop my hands to my sides. "Fine. What do you want to do?" I ask her. "Seriously, what? You want to leave? To head out in the storm?"

"The storm has slowed down. Stopped, even. It's safer out there than it is here, I just know it."

I sigh and lower my head. "Fine. Okay. Let's get our things, and we'll leave. If that's really what you want."

She looks so relieved as I say it I can't even be frustrated with her. As much as I want to believe her when she says something's wrong and trust her instincts, I can't help feeling like this is an overreaction. It wasn't that much blood on the floor—if it was even blood in the first place. I could've been wrong, I suppose. Exhaustion will do that to you. For all we know, someone spilled something. That's more likely, isn't it? It makes so much more sense.

Either way, apparently we're going to try to leave. Internally, I'm furious with myself for not taking the opportunity to sleep when I had it. It would've made things easier. To make it through this, I need to be aware of what's going on. Be alert.

And, at the moment, I'm the furthest thing from it.

We enter the motel room and gather our things, tossing our dirty clothes into my suitcase as I try and fail to find a way to convince her this is a terrible idea. I splash water over my face to help me wake up and brush my teeth while she uses the tiny bottle of mouthwash left on the counter.

I feel minutes away from death as my exhaustion kicks in, but there's no going back now.

"Were you bleeding again?" I ask, pointing toward her hand. There is blood in the cracks of her knuckles and under her fingernails. I don't remember that from before.

She looks down at her hands, eyes wide. "I, um...I don't know." She runs her hands under the water, washing them off. The water is dyed crimson just before it disappears down the drain. "This dry weather can make my skin crack sometimes." She chews her bottom lip, not meeting my eyes. It's as if she's lost in thought. "I don't think I touched the blood on the floor. It has to be mine." She holds her hand up, studying it. "The storm and the cold..." She's talking mostly to herself now, mumbling on and on.

I'm not sure I believe her, but what's the alternative? Clearly she didn't have anything to do with the blood in the lobby—she's much too freaked out by it—so what else could it be from?

"Maybe I scratched my leg in my sleep. The dry air makes me itchy, too, so it could've been that. There was blood on my leg when I woke up earlier." She pulls up the bottom of her sweatpants, and there is indeed quite a bit of dried blood smeared across her shin and calf. The wound has stopped bleeding from what I can tell, but it looks really deep. I'm still worried she's going to need stitches. "Yeesh," she mumbles. "That was it."

"Here, let me get you a washcloth to clean that up." I turn toward the shower and pull the curtain back.

The second I do, everything in my body turns to pure ice as she begins to scream. The sound of her cry fills my ears, a shrill shriek that seems to drown out all thoughts.

No.

I stare into the bathtub in utter shock. It's not possible. It can't be real. And yet, it is.

Ernest could just be taking a bath if there were any water in the tub. And, of course, if there wasn't blood dripping down his neck.

CHAPTER FIFTEEN

BEFORE

The coffee helps, but I'm still exhausted. Murder is tiresome business. Most people don't appreciate that enough. It's not just the physical aspect of it, the sheer brute strength it takes to stab someone hard enough for them to die, then drag their body to wherever you're going to lay them to rest. That's the easy part, really. That all comes before you've got to dig the hole.

Digging a grave is the single worst way to spend a day. Period. Don't let the movies fool you into thinking it can be done in just a few hours with only one or two swipes of a sweaty forehead.

At first, sure, it's not so bad. You get the first few shovelfuls of dirt, and it feels like everything will be okay. Like this time will be different than last. By the tenth shovelful, your arms start to burn if they aren't already. You begin to struggle with how to dig, whether to focus on making it wider or deeper, as neither seems to be working well. You lose track of time, your body burns and screams for you to stop, to rest, but you can't. You'll have to dig for hours upon hours, six or eight possibly, even when you're practiced at it. And that's when the ground isn't frozen. This time was so much worse, which was why I eventually had to give up and find another way. But not before breaking my back in the attempt.

Another tally in the con column for snowy murders.

I'm still undecided if I'll do it again.

You dig and you dig and you dig, and it's still not enough. Not nearly enough. For a human body especially, you have to get deeper than you think is possible and wide enough they can fit comfortably. And then there's the displaced dirt you have to find something to do with. And putting the grass back so it looks undisturbed. And the weeds. My god, the weeds. Cutting through weeds may as well be cutting through concrete.

It's not easy.

It's hard, laborious, thankless work.

It would've been easier if I could've buried them all, the two teenagers included. Safer. Less risky. If I'd had the space in my brain to consider it, I might have taken them to the woods for the animals, too, but I didn't. I wasn't thinking clearly, my mind muddled from exhaustion and adrenaline.

Even now, even from just partially digging the one grave for the one body, my arms burn. They feel like jelly every time I have to turn around a curve. I have dirt and blood caked under my fingernails. I desperately need a shower.

But it's done, and I'm satisfied.

I don't like to kill when I don't have to, but some people deserve to die. Not those kids, of course. Wrong place, wrong time. It couldn't be helped.

But him? He deserved it.

And that feels good.

Accomplished.

Like a hard day's work. And now, with him out of the way, I can enjoy my holiday.

Something draws my attention out of the corner of my eye up ahead, and I slow down. The car slides a bit as I hit the brakes, but it's okay.

Someone is there. Walking along the side of the road. A person with their hood up, not dressed nearly warm enough for this weather.

I should keep going, keep driving and pretend I didn't see them. The last thing I need is a distraction right now, but I can't help being intrigued.

Why would anyone be walking so late at night in this storm? And, if they're walking alone...would anyone miss them?

CHAPTER SIXTEEN

TIBBY

"He's dead," I whisper, my voice soft and breathless as I grab Walker's arm, pulling him back. I can't get out of here fast enough. I feel sick. I'm going to pass out. Going to die.

Like Ernest.

Ernest is dead.

Really, really dead.

His throat has been slashed. Quick, nasty work from the looks of it.

He's just...gone. He's gone.

Dead.

Blood has been smeared across the tub, but there's not a drop anywhere else in the bathroom. Everywhere I look, if there was any sign of him being brought in here, it's been cleaned up. Perhaps, then, he was killed in this room. In the bathtub, even. But if that's the case, why was there blood in the lobby? And why would he have been in our bathroom to have been killed here in the first place? He had no reason, and certainly no permission, to be in our room.

He's dead.

He's really freaking dead.

"The towels are gone," I whisper, noticing it for the first time. "Someone took the towels. Walker, the towels!"

I need him to look at me, to hear what I'm saying, but he isn't. Walker isn't looking at me, only at Ernest. His face is nearly as pale as the dead man's, his eyes wide.

"Walker, we need to call 9-1-1. *You* need to call 9-1-1." My heart pounds in my ears and, no matter how hard I try, I can't catch my breath. "Right now."

"I... I can try. I don't know if it will work." He glances down at his pocket, moving almost in slow motion.

"You said earlier that cell phones are supposed to work to call 9-1-1 even when there's no service."

"It's what I've always heard. I've never tried it to see if it works. In theory, if there's an active tower around, it should pick up the signal, even if it's not my network." He licks his lips and slips his hand into his pocket, pulling out his phone. He looks up at the bathtub again. At Ernest. His face pales.

"*Walker.*" My knees feel weak and I grab on to the wall for support.

"Sorry." He snaps his head back down to look at his phone and taps the screen to dial the three digits. The screen turns gray, signaling that the call is being placed, but before he can press the phone to his ear, the screen fades away with a soft *beep, beep* I can hear from where I stand.

Call Failed

My heart drops. No. No. No. It has to work.

"I'll try again," Walker whispers, tapping the number from his call log. He lifts the phone into the air, staring at the screen, but within seconds, he lowers it again, one corner of his mouth drawn in. "It's not working. It's supposed to connect to the nearest tower, but...they must all be out." He swallows and his eyes meet mine. The look he gives me is one of pure terror. "We can't even call 9-1-1."

I inhale deeply, refusing to look toward the bathtub again as ice swims in my veins. Deciding on a new course of action, I nod. "Okay. We have to go. We have to go right now."

He's still for a moment, studying me with that same look of horror. Then, snapping out of his trance, he turns around and nods. He follows me as I rush forward out of the room. As soon as we get a chance, as soon as we find a landline phone, we'll call the police and let them know, but for now, my instincts were right. Something bad is happening here, and if we stay, we'll be in danger.

"Why was he in our room?" Walker whispers from behind me. When I glance over my shoulder, his face is screwed up and contorted, obviously trying to make sense of something that could never make sense. "Why? How? How did he get in there? Did you let him in?"

I grimace, shaking my head. "What? No! Of course not. We were out of our room for a while. Someone could've put him in there."

Even as we're talking, a steady chorus is repeating in my brain.

He's dead.

He's dead.

He's dead.

"Who? Who would've put him in there? His wife?"

I swallow. "Maybe, I guess, but I doubt it. He said she was sick, remember? If that was her in the recliner, she certainly doesn't look capable of murder or of dragging him into the bathroom if she killed him somewhere else." Like the lobby, which is still my theory.

"Who then? It doesn't make any sense."

"I don't know. Maybe he, um...maybe *he* did it. You know, himself." I can't bring myself to say the words. "Or maybe it was one of the other guests."

"You said the man told you he saw him earlier. When was that? How long has he been...?"

I nod, chewing my bottom lip. "Right. He did. He did say he saw him. It was, I'm not sure how long ago. I'm... Everything happened so quickly." I stop talking as we get across the parking lot and stop in front of the car. Every hair on my arms stands on end as I stare at it, our only means of escape.

"No."

Both tires on my side have been slashed, right along with my hope that we were going to get out of here tonight.

"No," I repeat.

"Shit. Shit. Shit. Shit. *Shit!*" Walker rushes forward, circling the car and shaking his head. "All of them. Every single one."

"Try your phone again," I say, my voice low. Whoever did this could be anywhere. They could be watching us right now. "Try calling from out here. Outside."

He pulls out his phone and sets to work, but within seconds, he drops it to his side and shakes his head. "Nothing. It's not going through." He kicks the car angrily, cursing and dropping his head, chin to chest. He looks up, staring around with a new sense of urgency. "We have to find a phone that works. There has to be one somewhere. A landline. We can go into the lobby again and see if there's one on the desk. We could get the keys for every room and—"

"We don't have time for that. Most likely, none of them work anyway. We have to go *now*, Walker. Please." I'm dizzy. My head spins with possibilities as I slam into brick wall after brick wall in my mind. Nothing will work. Nothing will bring him back or erase the blood in the lobby. Nothing will fix his car or get us out of this mess. Nothing will make this horrible night go away.

I just want to wake up in my bed, safe and warm and cozy, and realize this has all been a bad dream.

"Yeah, of course, but how are we going to—" Before

he can finish the thought, a door shuts behind me, and I hear people talking. I spin around to find the man I saw earlier and a woman with brassy-blonde hair walking toward their car, too lost in conversation to notice us.

It's our only hope.

I rush forward. "Please. Can you give us a ride?"

The couple jumps back, grabbing hold of each other, clearly shocked to see me come out of nowhere.

"Oh! You scared me. We didn't see you there." The woman pats her hand against her chest, eyes wide. She's older than me by several years. Motherly, if not grandmotherly. Kind. I trust her in an instant. "I'm sorry. What did you say?"

"Our car tires were slashed and we need a ride." Walker gestures toward the car behind us. "Could you help us? I have cash. I can give you gas money. Whatever you need. We just have to get out of here."

"Slashed tires?" She looks over my shoulder at the car, then exchanges a wary glance with the man. "I don't know..."

"Where ya goin'?" The man eyes us suspiciously, his gaze bouncing between the two of us and the car.

"Literally wherever you will take us. We were on our way to St. Louis, but you can drop us off anywhere that's convenient on your way. We're desperate at this point. Please. We have no cell service, the phone lines here at the motel are down, and we just, we need to get out of here." I consider telling them about Ernest, but something inside my head warns me not to. If they know how serious the danger is, I worry they'll be in such a rush to get away from this place, they won't let us ride with them. Or, worse, they'll think we're dangerous.

"Cell towers do seem to be down." She gives us a sympathetic nod. "This place doesn't even have Wi-Fi. I keep trying to let my daughter know I'm okay, but I can't get a hold of her." She draws in one side of her mouth, studying us apprehensively.

Next to me, Walker pulls out a hundred-dollar bill and offers it to her. "Here. Please. To get us as far as you can. At least until we have service to call for help. Please. We have no other options. We're stranded here."

A slow puff of air escapes her lips. "Alright. Should we wake the other one, too?" She waves a hand toward the third room that appears to be occupied and the gray Toyota sitting in the parking lot. "Warn him? There was another man staying in that room. I saw him earlier. I don't think anyone else was with him, but I can't be sure. Maybe we should tell him we're leaving and warn him to keep an eye on his car if nothing else." The man she's talking about is the only guest we haven't seen. The light is still on inside his room, so it's possible he's awake. "Or we could wake the manager to see if he has security footage from the parking lot." She lifts her head, scanning the building for signs of a camera. "Maybe he could figure out who slashed your tires."

"No. We should just go." Walker takes a step toward me, placing a hand on my shoulder, and I know we're both thinking the same thing. If they go looking for

Ernest, there's a chance they'll find him. And, with his body in our bathroom, we'll look guilty as sin. "It's late, and they're both probably sleeping. I'll let my insurance company deal with it. We should get out of here before something worse happens."

"Worse than the tires?" The man's gray eyebrows dip together.

I nod. "Right. Worse than the tires." I'm surprised Walker hasn't told them about Ernest, but somehow, we seem to be in silent agreement. The less they know, the less we tell them, the better.

"Okay." The woman rests her hands on her hips with a huff. "Well, I suppose you can ride with us as long as you don't cause any trouble. It's the holidays, after all. I'd hope someone would give a ride to my daughter and her boyfriend if she needed it."

Walker removes his hand from my shoulder just as I say, "Oh, he's not my boyfriend."

The woman isn't paying attention. "Come on, kids. Get in before we all freeze to death out here."

"Thank you so much." I hurry toward the car as she opens the driver's door and gestures for me to follow her lead.

CHAPTER SEVENTEEN

WALKER

"I'll be right back," I tell Tibby, waving a hand at her as she slips into the back seat of the strangers' car. I try to slow my breathing. I'm doing my best to keep calm, to be stronger than I am so I don't scare Tibby, but it's not easy.

The image of Ernest's body flashes in my mind every time I close my eyes. The blood trickling down his neck, his lifeless, gray skin.

I hate that this is happening. Hate that she had to see him like that.

Squeezing my eyes shut, I shake my head, willing the thoughts away. There is no time to fall apart right now. I have to be quick about this. Tibby's waiting, and I don't want to scare her or leave her alone with them for too long. I lug my suitcase toward my car, my hands frozen solid on the handle, teeth chattering.

My mind is a mess as I flash back to pulling that

curtain aside and seeing the body again. Seeing her face as she stared at the body. Nothing about that was right.

Nothing about this whole situation is right.

He's just...dead. He's gone.

I wanted to protect her, and I've failed. I just wanted to find us a safe place to rest for the night, but instead, I've gotten us tied up in a murder with our DNA all over the crime scene.

And, though it's the least of my problems, I wanted to make it to my family's house for the holiday, but I won't. Every shred of my plans tonight have been torn apart.

And Ernest is dead.

And Tibby saw it.

And now we're going to ride with strangers because I fucked up.

I wish I could take it back. I wasn't thinking.

I'm tired. I'm so, so tired, and my body hurts, and I just need to sleep, but I can't because, more than anything else, I owe it to her to keep her safe.

This is all my fault.

What was I thinking?

I just don't understand how any of this could've happened. Things have gone so wrong, and I don't know how it's possible.

I pull open the car door with trembling hands, mindlessly grabbing a pack of gum from my center console and a pair of sunglasses from the visor. Nothing I'm doing makes sense and I'm aware of this, but I need to look like there was a reason for me to go to my car if she asks.

I lock the doors and make my way to the trunk, checking over my shoulder to be sure no one is watching.

I'm not sure what the road conditions are like, and I don't trust this woman's driving, but I can only hope we make it out of this. That we get somewhere with service and can call this in. I've never been more grateful we paid in cash and can potentially remain anonymous with our tip, though I suppose the car being in the parking lot puts a damper on those plans.

I pop open the trunk and stare at the bag of my nieces' Christmas gifts. I'd nearly forgotten about them in my rush to leave. I grab the bag with the gifts inside as my eyes land on the real reason I came back to the car. The one thing I can't leave here: the knife. The silver blade glints in the moonlight as I reach inside and close it. Checking over my shoulder one last time, I slip it into my pocket, then slam the trunk shut and head for the getaway car.

CHAPTER EIGHTEEN

TIBBY

We ride in complete and total silence. The couple doesn't speak to us or to each other. Walker doesn't speak to me. There is no music playing. Only the quiet sounds of the road and the snow and ice underneath our tires.

Partly, I assume it's because the woman is a cautious driver and wants to keep her mind clear on the roads, but partly, I think it's because she's keeping an eye on us and trying to decide if she's made a mistake by letting us ride with them. I squeeze my hands in my lap, shivering from the cold that seems to be seeping in from outside through the thin car windows and from the nerves currently wreaking havoc in my stomach.

I feel like a rubber band waiting to snap or a flame waiting to be snuffed out. Like I know something is coming, something is going to happen, but I don't know what.

I only know that I feel safer away from the motel,

though I can't get the image of Ernest's body out of my mind. The way he stared blankly into space, the way the blood was drying on his skin. Everything about that situation was wrong.

And his wife...

Oh, his poor wife. Alone in the chair. Sick. Helpless. Waiting for her husband to return with no idea that he won't. Will anyone ever care for her the way he did? Is she even conscious enough to understand what it means when he doesn't come back?

Even worse, she could be the one to find him.

Tears brim my eyes, and I force myself to think of anything else. I can't be weak right now. Ernest and his wife were strangers. For all I know, they were horrible people. I can't allow myself to grieve over them right now. I have to remain focused. To figure out a plan.

As soon as I find a phone, I'll call Jess. Well, no. I'll call the police first, then Jess. If she doesn't answer, I'll call my parents. They won't be happy about it, but I have to believe they'll come for me. They won't want me to be in danger, no matter how much of a disappointment I am to them.

Every once in a while, the man lowers his visor and stares at me in the mirror, his beady eyes gleaming in the glow from the stereo.

"Where are you kids from?" the woman asks, breaking the silence finally.

"Um, I'm staying near Atlanta right now." I tuck a piece of hair behind my ear, staring out the window. It'll take my parents hours to get here. I can only hope, wherever we stop, the place will be safe and warm. Maybe I'll end up at the police station, giving them my statement. But I don't know anything, really. I saw the blood, sure. And the trail leading toward the door. Will I get into trouble for not calling sooner?

Then again, how was I supposed to call when none of the phones were working? At least, *ours* wasn't. And neither was Walker's cell phone. I can't say for certain about the rest. Will they blame me for not checking all of them? What if the phone in the lobby was working and I could've called for help as soon as I saw the blood? Now that I think of it, was there even a phone in the lobby? I can't remember. What if it was only the phone in our room that was out? What if, by the time the police get there, that phone is back up and running, too, and I look like a liar? Or what if there was a code I wasn't aware of that I was supposed to dial first in order to place a call?

My thoughts and panic are dizzying.

"And you, honey?" The woman stares at Walker in the rearview.

"I live in South Carolina. A tiny little town." He runs a hand over his cheek. "But I have family on the Illinois side of St. Louis, which is where we're heading."

"How nice. Going home for the holidays, then?"

"Mm-hmm." Walker barely seems present in the conversation—either incredibly stressed or lost in thought. Perhaps seeing Ernest's body messed him up more than I realized at first. Neither of us could've prepared ourselves for that.

"We're just passing through." The woman reaches for the man's hand, kissing it lightly. "It's our honeymoon. Just got married."

"Congratulations." I force a smile.

She beams at the man in the seat beside her. "Thanks, doll. We were supposed to be going to Chicago to catch a flight for Aruba."

"Sounds nice. Anywhere warmer than here sounds pretty amazing right about now." I run a hand over the glass, tracing a pattern in the fog on the window.

"Would've been." The man grunts, adjusting in his seat as he lights up a cigarette and cracks his window so that from the back seat, we're getting pelted in the face with the smoke and cold air all at once. "If we weren't stuck in this hellhole."

"The storm came on fast," I agree. I look over in the seat next to me, unsure why Walker is being so quiet.

He's staring out the window, his head turned away from me.

"We pulled over to let it die off, but now that things have calmed down, we're hoping to still make it to the airport. Do you want to go all the way to Chicago with us? Maybe you could catch a flight to St. Louis from there. Or would you rather I just stop at the next gas station and drop you off?"

"The next gas station will be fine." Walker pulls out

his phone, staring down at it. He opens the screen to his call log and tries to call 911 again. I hold my breath.

Call Failed

"If there is one," he adds, locking his screen with a sigh. "I just need to find someplace with cell service or a landline we can use to call for help."

"There should be a store or gas station once we get into town. I imagine most places have closed down from the storm, though." She clicks her tongue as we near a city limit sign. "Oh, here we go. We're coming into a town now, it looks like. Help me keep an eye out for a good place to drop you off."

In almost perfect unison, Walker and I turn to look out our windows and search for not just a *good* place, but *any* place that seems open in the sleepy little town.

"Everything looks closed to me." The man puffs out the last of his cigarette, tossing the butt out the window before rolling it up.

She sighs, tapping her fingers on the steering wheel. "Well, that's what I was worried about. It's okay. We'll figure it out. I don't think there's much here, but I'm sure we can find you kids someplace that's open or that has a pay phone outside if nothing else." She falls silent as we search for a place, driving past one closed store after another. With another deep breath, she adds, "Things sure were easier back in the days when there were pay phones on every corner. I know everyone loves their cell phones nowadays, but when something like this happens, look where it leaves us. No one has any way to contact anyone else. "

The main street running through the town is a solid sheet of white. There are no lines to be seen and no other cars on the road. The traffic lights are out, blinking red, and every single place we pass has been shut down, either for the night or because of the storm. Either way, finding somewhere that's open is beginning to feel impossible.

"Oh, dear. We might have better luck in another town. I don't think it hit up north like it did here," she says. "Will you guys be okay riding with us a little while longer? Just a few hours north, and things'll be easier. The bigger cities all still seem to have pay phones and, with any luck, we could end up with enough cell phone service not to need it. Of course, that could be wishful thinking on my part. My daughter must be so worried—"

"*Wait!*" Walker shouts suddenly, causing the woman to slam on her brakes. The car jerks forward, sliding rather than stopping, and she curses.

"Oh, shoot! Shoot! Sorry! I'm sorry!" Her hands fly up into the air as if she's surrendering.

Panic seizes in my chest, my entire body rigid as I brace myself for impact. *No. No. No. No. No.*

"Pump the brakes!" the man shouts at her, reaching for the steering wheel.

"I am! *I'm pumping, I'm pumping!*" She snaps her hands back onto the steering wheel, eyes wide. Slowly, the car comes to a stop against a curb, and she lets out a loud sigh of relief. "Is everyone alright?" She whips her head around to look at us, and we nod. "I'm so sorry."

"I'm fine," I tell her, running a hand along my body as if to assure us both. I glance over at Walker. "We're both fine."

She puffs out another sigh of relief, brushing her hair back from her face. "I really didn't think we were going to stop." Glancing in the rearview mirror, she eyes Walker. "You screamed, and I just panicked. Is everything alright? What was the matter?"

"There's a pay phone," Walker says, pointing to the store parking lot to our right. I follow his finger's path, realizing he's right. "I barely saw the sign in time. I didn't want us to pass it." He pats his pockets. "Does anyone have any change? I didn't even think about looking for coins in my car before we left, and I never carry any in my wallet."

The woman opens the center console. "I do. Tony, can you find them some quarters in here? I'm sure there are a few."

The man—*Tony*, apparently—begins digging in the console while the woman navigates the car slowly to the edge of the parking lot. "I don't think I can get in there." Her voice is quiet and apologetic. "It looks bad. I'm afraid I'll get us stuck, and we won't be able to get back out. The parking lot is nothing but ice."

"I can make it from here. It's fine," Walker says as Tony drops two dollars worth of quarters into his palm.

"Don't know how much you need. That should get ya by."

"Thanks, this is perfect." He looks my way. "Come with me?"

I nod and push open my door. "Yeah. Of course." It's funny how much can change in a single night. In less than a few hours, really. When I first met Walker, I couldn't stand him and definitely didn't trust him. Now, I can't imagine staying in the car without him.

"We'll be right here, you two," the woman promises, waving at us like we're boarding a train and will never see her again. "Bundle up, okay? And hurry. I don't want you guys to freeze out there."

"We'll be back." Walker slides toward me.

Together, we step out of the car on my side. The woman wasn't wrong. The parking lot is nothing but ice. I slip and slide with every step on our way up the hill toward the pay phone. Walker holds out his arm, and I reluctantly grasp onto him when I realize my only other option is falling on my face. We move slowly and cautiously.

"Thank goodness you saw this." I'm out of breath as the cold air burns my lungs.

"Yeah, I just happened to."

"Are you okay?" I glance over at him, then squeeze my eyes shut and look away. "Stupid question. Of course you're not okay. How could either of us be? Seeing Ernest like that..."

His hand squeezes my arm, and he gives a slight,

sharp jerk of a nod. "I just can't believe he ended up there. I can't believe I left you in that room. If anything had happened to you while I was gone..."

"I'm fine." I bump my head against his shoulder. "Honestly. Totally fine. Not even a scratch on me."

"Did you use the bathroom when you woke up? Were you in there to see if the bathtub was empty then? So we could decide if...you know, if he was in there before you woke up or after."

"No." I eye him. "Did you? I mean, before you left?"

"I never went to sleep. No one was in that room while I was there." He pulls me tighter to him as we make the final push up the hill. "Careful, this part seems extra slippery." Just as he says it, he loses his balance. "Oh! Oh! Careful. Careful." He swings his arm, pulling me against his chest with the other, and the two of us begin to topple over together. I squeeze my eyes shut, outstretching my hand and bracing for the moment when we'll hit the ground, but somehow, he manages to steady us just in time.

"Careful," he says again, his voice soft. He strokes my arm gently with his hand, though he seems almost unaware he's doing it. My heart races in my chest.

"You okay?" I check on him, and he nods.

"In terms of not falling and busting my face on the ice, yes. I'll just feel better once we've talked to the police. I can't stop thinking about his wife. She's going to wake up and realize he's not there. That he's never coming back." He looks away.

"I know. I was thinking the same thing."

"It must be nice." His voice is a soft whisper. "To have someone who loves you like that."

I smile but don't say anything else. I guess there's nothing really left to say.

We reach the front of the parking lot, and Walker drops his arm away from me. The grocery store is small and dark inside, with only the entrance lit up.

"Here's hoping this works," Walker says when we finally reach the phone. He drops four quarters into the slot and jabs his shaking fingers into the buttons for 911. After a few moments, his eyes widen. "Yes, hello. We need help at the motel off of, erm..." He pauses, thinking. "Oh. Highway thirty-seven, I think. I'm nearly positive that was it. It's a red building with just a few rooms." Another pause. "Well, I don't know what it was called. There wasn't a sign. It's just outside of...um, Goreville, I think was the name of the town we passed through. Super small. Run by a guy named Ernest, but he's...he's dead." He swallows, looking down. "So we need your help."

I grip his arm and rub a hand over his back, hoping to reassure him I'm here.

"My name?" he goes on. "Walker Whitlock. I tried to call earlier from my cell phone, but the call wouldn't go through no matter what I did." He pauses. "I was staying there tonight, yes. Along with a few other guests. But now we're leaving because we don't feel safe and... Okay. Um, sure." He glances at me with a nervous look. "How long will that be? Well, we're already in…" He looks around. "I have no idea where we are. We're at, er, well, the sign just says grocery. Can you see the address I'm calling from? I'm sorry, none of us are from around here. The storm rerouted us, and we don't have cell service, like I mentioned, also because of the storm, and we got a ride from someone—another guest— because our tires were slashed." He eyes me, listening to whatever is being said on the other end of the line. "No, I mean, I don't think anyone there had a weapon. There's only one other guest staying there who we didn't meet, but I never saw them. The people we're traveling with said it was a man on his own. I didn't ask much else, but they can tell you more if you talk to them. Or if the police do. Okay. Okay." He pauses. "Okay."

He ends the call, placing the phone down slowly. "She said landlines, cell towers, and power are out all across the region. It's lucky we were able to find one that worked, but…um, they want us to go back to the motel to meet the police."

My heart flutters in my chest. "What? We can't go back."

"I know, but she didn't really give me a choice."

"Walker, it's not safe. Couldn't the police come here?"

He runs a hand through his hair, looking everywhere but at me. "With the storm, I think they're trying to limit travel even for the officers. She just said they'll want us on scene for questioning. She didn't give me an option for them to meet us here. I didn't know what else to do."

"Okay, but who knows if they'll even take us back." I gesture toward the car waiting near the entrance to the parking lot. "They were nice enough to bring us here. We can't ask them to go back and miss their honeymoon."

He nods. "Yes, we can. We don't have a choice, and neither do they. They have to go back, too. They're suspects as much as we are."

"Suspects?" I repeat the word, my stomach feeling hollow.

In the car, the woman and Tony are staring at us. The overhead light illuminates their faces as they watch us with strange expressions. Waiting to see what will happen. What we're doing. Why it's taking so long.

They still have no idea what happened at the motel other than the tires being slashed. To tell them the truth, admit that we lied to them, feels impossible. Nausea washes over me.

"Come on." Walker holds out his hand, and I slip mine into it, letting him lead us back to the car slowly, gripping on to my arm too tightly to keep me from falling.

Back at the car, we slide inside, and Walker tells them what the dispatcher said.

"No. We ain't going back," Tony argues with a thick southern accent. "We barely made it here. No way in hell are we going back."

"We have a flight to catch." The woman winces,

cocking her head to the side. "I'm sorry, kids, but he's right." She gives me a sympathetic look. "I get it, I really do, but I just don't see what your slashed tires have to do with us. We'll give you our information for the police if they want to call us, but we didn't see anything. We have a flight to catch, and I'll just be sick if we miss it. We've been saving for months."

Walker and I exchange a glance. They still think this is all about the tires. We have to tell them the truth about Ernest.

I open my mouth to do just that when Walker says, "You know what? I agree. We shouldn't wait. Whoever *did this*"—his eyes meet mine with extra meaning in the words, the killer, not the tire slasher, though they're likely one and the same—"is still out there. If we go back, we could be in danger. They can't blame us for not being able to make it back to the motel with roads the way they are. We barely made it here. We did what we needed to by calling and reporting it. The rest is up to them."

"But you gave them your name. They'll find your car. What if you get in trouble for fleeing a crime scene?" I ask.

His brows draw down. "I doubt it's considered fleeing if I'm the one who reported it," he says, though he doesn't look sure. "If our ride won't take us back, how are we supposed to get there?"

"We should go call the police again, then." I chew the inside of my cheek. Force of nervous habit. "At least we need to tell them that we aren't coming back and why. I don't want you to get in trouble."

Our eyes lock, darting back and forth between each others', carrying on a silent conversation in the back seat. I don't like the idea of not going back, but it suddenly feels like it's three against one. I'm only looking out for Walker, really, though I have no idea why. There's nothing at all that will connect me to the motel or the crime scene. I should just leave and never look back. Whatever happens is on him, not me.

"Look, kids, we really need to get going." The woman interrupts my racing thoughts, turning in her seat to look at me. "We need you to let us know whether we're leaving you or you're coming with us. I'm sorry, but we can't keep waiting. We've already been slowed down quite a bit, and we'll be pushing it to make it to Chicago in time to catch our flight."

"Give us just a second, please," Walker says, nudging me back out of the car. We shut the door, and he looks down at me. "Look, I need you to be honest with me. Are you running from something? Or from someone?"

"What?" I furrow my brows, staring at him with confusion swimming in my head.

He presses his lips together and stares over my head. "Earlier, when we talked about the police, you were clearly freaked out and didn't want to call them. Now you're all about it. What changed? Why didn't you want to call them before? Why were you in such a hurry?"

A brick settles in my stomach. I hesitate.

He lowers his head slightly, his eyes drilling into mine. "No lies, remember? We had a deal."

I pinch the skin on the bridge of my nose. "It's stupid. I was... It doesn't really matter anymore. Not after all of this. It's just that, well, I didn't tell you, but my, um, my ex is a cop. I didn't, um... I didn't want it to get back to him somehow. I don't know how it all works or what he'd find out, if he'd find anything out, but I was so angry with him, I *am* so angry with him, I didn't want him to know where I was or that I'd needed help. I wanted to have made it on my own. And I wanted to keep moving until I was somewhere safe with my friends, somewhere with enough service to contact my family and tell them the truth before he could put his own spin on what happened. Before he could make it look like I was crazy or irrational or that this was somehow all my fault. Before he could turn everyone against me. He's... He's charming like that." Thinking of him, I zone out, then snap back to the present. "But none of that matters now. Someone *killed*"—I whisper the word—"Ernest. We have to tell the police what we know. If we don't, you could get in big trouble, and that's the last thing I want after you are only in this mess because you tried to help me."

"That's not true."

"We both know you'd be a lot farther along if you hadn't had to stop for me. You said it yourself earlier."

He scowls. "Forget what I said earlier. I want you somewhere safe." His hand comes to rest on my arm.

"Nothing else matters right now. Leaving with them, heading to Chicago or St. Louis or wherever, as long as it's far away from here, feels like the safest bet."

"But what about the police?"

"They told us to come back, but if we don't have a way, what are we supposed to do? We'll call them once we're somewhere safe and explain everything. I'll handle it, don't worry. Right now, our safety is a priority, and I think they'll understand that."

The window rolls down, and Tony sticks his head out. "What's the verdict? You comin', or what?"

"We're coming," Walker says, and I don't argue. In truth, I'm not sure why I don't, except that maybe I want to trust him.

"Alright, then you're with us 'til Chicago. This has to be the last stop for a while. That cool?"

"We just need to get out of here." Walker takes my hand.

Tony steps out of the car, gesturing toward us. "Alright. First things first, though. If you're riding with us that far, I wanna search you for weapons."

CHAPTER NINETEEN

WALKER

"You've gotta be fucking kidding me." I stare at Tony in disbelief. "No. No. Absolutely not. You're not going to touch us. What have we done that makes you suddenly suspicious of us? We've ridden all this way and not caused any issues."

"Maybe so, and I'm sorry, but I gotta protect my lady." His eyes trail the length of Tibby's body, and I see red. "Gotta check and make sure we're all safe. Your bags, too."

"Like hell. We've ridden with you all this time, and you've been fine. If you don't want us to ride any farther, just say that."

"Chicago's a lot farther than an hour up the road. Now, either let me check you and let's get going, or say no, and we'll leave. Either way, it's up to you, but you have to decide now."

"You aren't touching her," I tell him firmly, stepping in front of Tibby.

"I don't have anything," she says, lifting her shirt so we can see her bare stomach. "No weapons." She pulls up her sleeves and pant legs, then flips out the waist of her pants. "I'm not a danger to you."

He steps forward, reaching out a hand to feel in between her legs. I lunge forward, but she holds out a hand to stop me, her eyes blank as she shakes her head. "It's okay. Just...just let him."

It's not. It's not okay. It's the furthest thing from okay. I want to rip him to pieces. Thankfully, though, he stops at a respectable place just above her knees and, seeming satisfied, steps back. "Thanks, sweetheart."

Next, he turns to me, and I know what he'll find as he pats my jeans. As soon as his fingers touch the outline of the knife, his eyes light up and he gives me a questioning look before sticking his hand into my pocket. I groan as he pulls out the knife and holds it up in the air.

His eyes zero in on it. "What's this?"

"A pocketknife, clearly."

Beside me, Tibby tenses. I reach for her arm, but she pulls it away. I know what she must think of me, what she must now think she knows and understands, and I want so desperately to explain it all, but not in front of him.

"Why do you have it?" Tony turns the knife over in his hands, running a finger across the metal.

I shrug one shoulder. "I don't know. I always carry one. It's just a dull blade. No big deal."

He moves to tuck it into his pocket.

At once, I reach for it. "Hey! Give it back."

He shakes his head. "You can have it back when we get you where you're going."

"And if *you're* a danger to *us*?" I demand. "You're leaving me with nothing to protect ourselves."

"It's your choice to ride with us." Tony runs his tongue over his teeth. "Our car, our rules." I want to tell him to forget it, to give me the knife back and leave us here, but it's not an option. I can't risk keeping Tibby out in this cold much longer.

He finishes patting me down, being extra thorough now, though there's nothing else to find except my phone which he allows me to keep. When he's done, he pulls my suitcase and the bag of gifts out of the car and searches them painstakingly, tossing my things all around and tearing open the gifts one by one.

I'm fuming as I watch him inspect the box of the veterinarian Barbie doll my niece has been begging for, then toss it aside. My body radiates with anger as he rips the wrapping paper off the last gift and examines it, his wrinkled lips set in a thin line underneath his gray mustache.

When he's done with the searching and otherwise humiliating us, he stuffs my clothes back into the suitcase and the gifts back into their bag, then places both bags into the trunk of the car, out of my reach.

I gesture toward the trunk as he slams it closed. "If you were going to put them back there, why did you have to search them in the first place? It's not like I can get to them from the back seat."

"Can't be too careful," he says, wagging a finger at me with a wry grin.

I'm so angry my entire chest feels like a ball of fire, like I'll be ready to explode at a moment's notice. I want nothing more than to steal my knife back, grab Tibby, and make a run for it.

I don't trust these people not to hurt her, and now I have no way to defend us should things go wrong.

Without another word, he slips back into the car and places my knife in the center console, patting the top for good measure.

I reach for Tibby and keep my voice low. "I can explain."

"Did you do it?" Her voice shakes as she asks the question, and it kills me.

"Of course not."

"We gotta get moving, kids." The woman stares at us impatiently, her voice carrying through Tony's open door.

Tibby opens the back door, easing inside the car. "Let's just go, Walker."

I open my mouth to say more, but she closes the door at once and Tony shuts his as well, cutting me off. I move around to the other side of the car and slide in. Once inside, the woman stares over her shoulder at us with a pained expression. "I'm sorry about all that, but you know you can never be too careful. Are you both okay, temperature-wise?" Tibby nods. "Let me know if it gets too hot or too cold back there. I'm Lori, by the way. I don't think I ever said that. And this is my husband, Tony." When we don't respond, she prompts, "What are your names?"

"Tibby." She doesn't look at me. *Refuses* to look at me. I don't want to imagine what awful scenarios must be running through her head right now. She thinks she knows what I've done, but I need to explain. I *can* explain if she'll just give me the chance. "And this is Walker." My name on her tongue drips with venom.

Lori eases the car off the shoulder of the road, pointing us out of town. Slowly, we start on our journey, and I have a feeling it's going to be a long, miserable ride.

From where I sit, I hang my head down, furious over what's just happened. I don't go anywhere without my grandpa's pocketknife, but if this is the only way to keep Tibby safe, I guess it's what I'll do. I can't leave her alone with them. I don't trust anyone with her, even if she no longer trusts me. Still, I won't feel calm again until the knife is safely back in my pocket where it belongs.

"You kids will be so relieved to get home to your families, I'm sure. They must be thrilled to have you home for the holidays. Which of your families are you visiting first? It can always be so difficult to navigate those sorts of things. You know, who are we seeing first? Who will we spend the most time with? My first husband

and I had so much trouble with that." She adjusts her rearview mirror, looking at Tibby in the reflection. Despite her earlier silence, Lori is obviously a talker, though I wish she'd shut up. Then again, I'm grateful for the distraction as I try to decide how to explain everything.

"Oh, we aren't together." Tibby is quick to correct her. "Walker just...well, he picked me up tonight after I, um, well... I just needed a ride, and he was there." Her head turns to look at me, and I try to meet her eyes, but just as quickly, she looks away. It's as if she didn't realize she was doing it. "We're just traveling together. We don't know each other at all, really." She glances out the window, then adds, seemingly to drive the point home further, "We only met a few hours ago. He was supposed to take me to a gas station so I could call a friend, but the storm closed the interstate, so we got stuck together."

My throat goes dry over the obvious way she wanted to make that known. That we aren't together. That we never will be. That she's only with me now because the weather forced us to be together. That she'd rather be anywhere else.

The couple exchanges a knowing look, and I suspect they're thinking about how we were sharing a room and assuming this is some sort of weird one-night stand.

Let them think what they want.

I run my feet under their seat, checking for anything else I could use as a weapon should the need arise.

"Well, it sure is lucky he found you, then. This storm

is brutal. I'm hoping we've already seen the worst of it," Lori says, reaching forward to adjust the heat.

"I hope so, too," Tibby says.

"I always liked snow," Tony tells us, his voice whimsical. "Snow days when I was a kid, building snowmen. Snowball fights. Even now, I love it and wish we'd get more snow."

"Only when we don't have to travel in it," Lori says pointedly.

"Of course." He slips his hand across the center console and takes hers, lifting her knuckles to his lips and pressing a kiss to each one.

While she's busy asking Tibby something else about her travels, I stick my hand into the pocket on the back of the seat carefully. Every move feels noisy, and I can only hope no one notices what I'm doing.

If I could just find a pen or a lighter, a book, even. Something heavy. Just something to protect us in case things go badly.

My hand connects with something thin. Paper, I suppose. Useless. I pull it out anyway and stare down, and suddenly, my blood runs cold. I blink rapidly, trying to clear my eyes and make sense of what I'm seeing.

What the...

"Everything okay?" Tibby whispers, leaning over to see what I'm looking at.

I shove the photo down to my side. "No. I, uh, I'm going to be sick." I'm not so sure it's a lie. I feel lightheaded. "I'm going to be sick right now. Pull over."

"What?" Lori adjusts the heat so it's not blowing as hard and she can hear us better. "What's wrong? You're getting carsick? Should I crack a window?"

I cover my mouth. "No. Let me out of the car. Now. Please pull over."

She slows the car to a quick, messy stop, and I fall out of my side, crawling across the wet snow toward Tibby's side of the vehicle. She opens her door and stares down at me as if she thinks I've lost my mind.

Maybe I have. It would make more sense than what I suspect. What I now know.

Then again, no it wouldn't, because suddenly, everything makes perfect sense. The picture forms in my mind with total clarity.

"What are you doing?" she shouts, waving a hand in my direction. "Get back in the car."

I reach for Tibby's hand, standing to my feet. "Come on." I pull her, practically dragging her farther away. I'm half surprised she's coming with me, shocked she isn't refusing to listen to me now that she thinks I'm dangerous. I can only take that as a good sign. She must still trust me a little bit, even if she hates herself for it.

"What are you talking about?" She jerks her hand from my grasp. "What's happening? What's wrong?" She digs her feet into the snow, refusing to move another inch until I explain what's going on. "Tell me what you're freaking out about."

"I..." I don't even know how to explain it. There's no possible way to put this into words without making her think I'm absolutely insane. Either that, or I'm lying to get her to trust me again. Thinking quickly, I shove the picture into her hand and drop to the ground, facing away from the car as Tony and Lori step out.

"What's happening?" Tony shouts, cupping his hands around his mouth.

"Are you alright, hon?" Lori stands on her tiptoes, trying to get a better look from where they're standing just a few feet away. "Did you get carsick?"

I wave away their questions. From the ground, hunched over as if I'm getting sick, I'm not listening. I'm only looking at Tibby as she stares down at the photo with wide eyes full of every question running through my own mind.

I know from the look on her face I'm not wrong. That she understands what it is, just the same as I did. The graduation portrait in her hand is of the unmistakable face of the boy from the news. The boy who went missing, whose family hasn't heard from him in hours. The one Tibby worried was somehow connected to the motel.

Now I'm worried she might have been right.

I hope with everything in me, she understands that this must mean what I think it means. When she looks up at me finally, her jaw is slack.

"Is this...?"

She doesn't have to finish the question. I nod and swallow.

"Walker..."

"I know."

She looks down at the photo again. "Where did you find this?"

"It was in the pocket on the back of the seat."

"And you think it means—"

"I think it means exactly what you're thinking, Tibby." I take the photo from her, willing her to look up at me. When she does, I say the words that need to be said. Need to be processed and comprehended so we can move forward with our new reality. "Lori and Tony have been lying to us. This isn't their car. The car we're riding in belonged to the missing boy from the news. And I'd bet anything they know what happened to him."

CHAPTER TWENTY

BEFORE

It takes longer than usual to slow the car to a stop thanks to the road conditions, and the person in the hooded jacket clearly doesn't want to be picked up, but it certainly beats the alternative, doesn't it?

As I stop the car fully, I roll down the window and shout, "Hey! Are you okay?"

The person stops in their tracks. Their jeans are soaking wet at the bottom from the snow. They turn around slowly, and in the shadows, I can't see their face until they lower the hood.

When he does, I get a better look at him. Greasy, gray hair, a round belly. A thick mustache.

He slowly walks back to the car and bends down to look at me, releasing a loud whistle. "Well, you sure are a sight for sore eyes."

I giggle at the obvious attempt to flirt. "Thanks. Are

you okay? The storm is supposed to get bad tonight. Can I give you a ride anywhere?"

"Nah. Thanks, sweetheart. I just live around the corner," he says. "Walked down to check my neighbor's mail while they're out of town."

"Do you want a ride home? I don't mind."

He opens his mouth, then closes it again, clearly reconsidering his answer. "Are you sure?"

I search for the button to unlock the car, still learning how this thing works. "Yeah, absolutely. Hop in."

"Ah, I appreciate it." He opens the door, sliding into the passenger seat with a shiver. "It sure feels better in here than it does out there. This storm is gonna be a doozy. I don't trust our weathermen, you know? Only job in the world where you can be wrong half the time and not get fired." He chuckles. "So I never know what to expect until it's here."

"Totally."

"You from around here?"

"Nope, just passing through. My husband and I were supposed to be on our anniversary trip to Aruba, but I found out he'd been cheating, so I'm taking it alone."

He stares at me. "I'm awful sorry to hear that, darlin'."

"Thanks." I start up the car, easing it forward. "Buckled in?"

He buckles up slowly, easing the seat belt around his belly. "No one should have to take a trip like that alone.

And, I hope you don't mind me saying it, he's a fool for lettin' you go."

I smile at him. "You're sweet."

"It's the truth."

I glance over at him, spotting an opportunity when I see it. Too many bodies here wouldn't be good for me. I need some space from this area, but that doesn't mean I can't bring my next easy target along. "You know...maybe this is crazy..." I feign shyness. "No. Forget it. Never mind."

He smiles at me broadly. "What is it, honey?"

"No, nothing. You'd think it's silly."

"I won't. Try me."

"Well, I hope you don't think awful of me, but I have another ticket. I know we're strangers and all, but I mean, if you don't have plans for the holiday, would you maybe want to tag along?"

He hesitates. "Oh. Well, that's real nice of ya, but I don't know."

"I swear I'm not crazy," I say with a laugh. "It could be fun. Way more fun than going alone. Unless you're married or something?" I already noticed his ring finger is bare, but I pretend I didn't check.

"Nah, nah. Ain't married. Tried that once. Didn't last." He runs a hand over his mustache, smoothing it down as he thinks.

"See." I nudge him with my elbow. "It could be fun. Just a week out of this snow. All free. You don't have to pay for anything. We'll stop by your house and grab a bag on our way. And then I'll drop you off at home on my way back." I reach for his hand. "It would just be one week of adventure. How often do you get that?"

He's quiet for a while, studying me out of the corner of his eye like he thinks it might be a prank.

"Come on. Please? You could pretend to be my husband. We could act like we're on our honeymoon, get all sorts of free things. What could be more fun?"

He sighs. "You're really serious about this, aren't you?"

"I've never been more serious in my life." I wink. "I need a friend this week, and you seem like a good friend."

His lips twist in thought. "I'm supposed to be checking my neighbor's mail."

"It's just mail," I tell him. "Live a little."

He's quiet for a while, but eventually a smile spreads to his lips. "What'd you say your name was again?"

"I didn't," I remind him. "But it's Lori."

He holds out a hand out. "Nice to meet you, Lori. I'm Tony."

CHAPTER TWENTY-ONE

TIBBY

I stare down at the photo of the boy. There's a frame designed around it, which says "Class of 2023." He just graduated this year. He was supposed to have his whole life ahead of him. He was probably coming home for the holidays, maybe to introduce his parents to his new girlfriend.

Now both of them are missing. Their car has been stolen.

Most likely, they're both dead.

Just like Ernest.

His face flashes through my mind again.

His poor wife.

"If this is his car, Tibby, it means they stole it. For whatever reason. Maybe they stole it and left them stranded or..." Walker keeps his voice low as he explains it to me as if I might not get it. "Maybe not."

"I know," I say gently, not needing further explanation. "What do we do? How do I know I can trust you?" That idea ricochets through me. He could be lying. He could've gotten this photo anywhere.

I can't mistake the hurt in his eyes. "I think you know you can."

"I thought I could, too. Until the knife."

"I can explain that—"

"What's going on?" Lori shouts, moving closer to us.

"He's sick," I call over my shoulder, panic surging in my gut. I don't want to be alone with her. I don't want to be away from Walker. I shouldn't trust him, but there's no denying I do. "Give us a minute."

"It was him, Tibby," he says. "Them, maybe. Either way, we have to go."

"Could they have killed Ernest, too?" It's all coming together in my mind. "Tony told me he saw him, that he'd come to fix something in their room, but that gave them time to plant the body."

He nods. "I think so. It has to be them." Wiping his mouth with the back of his hand, he glances over my shoulder. "*No!* Tibby, look out!"

I turn to find Lori lunging for us, much closer than I expected. I scream, but my body freezes with fear. The knife she has in her hand isn't the one they took from Walker. It's larger, with a thick, black handle.

Leaping into action, Walker shoves me aside just in time for the knife to narrowly miss my back. Lori collides with him, and they roll on the ground, their bodies a tangled mess in the snow as he tries to fight her off.

"Walker!" I shout, pushing up to my feet.

In an instant, Tony is running over, too. "What the hell are you doing?" he shouts at her, hands on both sides of his face. "Lori, stop! Why are you... What are you..." The horror in his expression is obvious. Whatever is happening right now, I truly don't think he's involved. Either that, or whatever their plan was, she has completely gone against it. He doesn't seem to know what his wife is capable of or why she's attacking us, and neither do I. All I can assume is that she knows what we now know. Tony covers his mouth, his voice shaking as he begins to back away, heading for the car.

"The knife." I race forward, shouting at him, "Stop! Help us! We need Walker's knife!"

He stares at me, then at her, continuing to back away. Walker shoves her off, pushing to his feet and trying to run away, but she matches him step for step as he makes his escape.

He looks over his shoulder, his eyes locking with mine, and she rears her arm back. I watch in a horrified stupor, screaming out moments too late as the knife plunges into his back.

He stops at once, stunned by the injury, freezing up as if he's run into an invisible wall. She pulls the knife back and shoves it into him again.

I don't even realize I'm screaming until the sounds of my wails bring me back to reality.

I bend at my waist, emptying what little remains in my stomach onto the white snow.

When I look up, his entire body convulses with the impact of yet another blow. She's methodical about the way she stabs him, emotionless even. It takes nothing from her but everything from him. Everything from me.

His fall to the ground is softened by the snow, and when she turns toward Tony and me, I scramble backward, breathless from the loss, weak from fear. My body trembles from vomiting, and my ears are ringing.

"What did you do, Lori?" Tony asks, shaking his head. He's trying to pull open the car door, but I realize it must be locked. He's just as trapped as we are, and now I'm positive he's not involved in this plan. He looks as though he's going to pass out. "Why would you do that?" He's crying, I realize, and I'm aware that I am, too. Cold, wet tears paint my cheeks as I watch her approach him without a word. "*Why?*" he demands.

"Tony..." She holds both arms out as if she might drop the knife, though she doesn't. "Wait, Tony. Please! Just wait. Let me explain. I had to do it. I had to."

For a second, I'm not sure what she's doing, but then I realize she's going to pull him into a hug as she crosses the snowy ground quickly on her way to him. He seems frozen in place as he lets her approach him, still crying and shaking.

"Why?" he asks again through his tears, his voice soft.

"Shhh..." She silences him as she moves closer. "Come here."

No time to waste, I rush forward across the snow banks and to Walker as fast as my legs will carry me.

When I reach him, I drop down on my knees next to where he's lying. His blood is slowly painting the snow crimson all around him.

I place a hand on his back. "Walker..."

His eyes flick open at the sound of my voice. He's still alive, but barely. His chest rises and falls with quick, ragged breaths. He clutches a handful of snow under his palm, his eyes wild as he searches the night sky for something I don't understand.

I dig into his pocket and find his phone, dialing 911. *"Please. Please. Please. Please. Please."*

Call Failed

I try again.

Call Failed

And again.

Call Failed

And again.

Each time, I get the same horrible message. The message that tells me help isn't coming. That we're on our own.

He lifts his hand slowly, reaching for the phone and slips it out of my grasp.

"No. Stop it. I'm not giving up on you," I vow, taking it back from him. His hand comes to rest on my thigh and fresh tears sting my eyes.

"It's okay." His voice is powerless. Empty.

I can't watch him die, but I can't look away.

I should go. I should run. I should leave him and save myself, and yet I can't move. I don't even want to.

"Walker." My tears fall onto his shirt, painting dark speckles on the fabric. "I'm so sorry. What do I do? What should I do?" The storm's repercussions are endless. I have no phone and no way to call for help. No vehicle. Nothing. I'm alone, and he's dying, and there's absolutely nothing I can do about it.

I want to say so much. To thank him for all he did for me, to tell him how much it's meant, how much he means, but I can't bring myself to say the words. Even in this terrible, heart-wrenching moment, the last moment I may get with him, I can't push past the uncomfortable feeling of vulnerability. I guess he was right. I'm a cat through and through. And my dog, my best friend, is dying right in front of me.

"You have to run. You have to leave me." His voice is broken and powerless as he flips his hand over, fingers outstretched.

He's reaching for me.

The Tibby he met earlier tonight wouldn't have taken his hand for all the money in the world. In fact, she would've slapped it away for good measure. But now, this version of myself...I can't help it. I don't want to resist. A lump forms in my throat, so sticky and thick I can't swallow it down. If that's all I can do, the only way I can show him how much he means to me, I'll do it. I take his hand and hold it between both of mine, hoping he'll somehow understand what I'm trying to say. What I wish I was strong enough to say.

"I'm not leaving you," I promise him. Hours ago, we

were strangers. Now, the idea of losing him is devastating. Painful in the most real, raw way imaginable.

I won't survive watching him die. I know this as much as I know I need oxygen to live, and yet I refuse to leave him or look away. I need to save him. I'd do anything to save him, but it's impossible.

The realization sits heavily in my chest. There's guilt there, too, because if the situation were reversed, he'd probably do something stupid like attack Lori and steal the car, somehow making it to the hospital just in time to save me.

But I can't do that.

"Grr-ugh." I hear the noise from behind me and spin just in time to see Tony collapse on the ground, the red line on his neck dripping the way Ernest's had.

Lori turns back to me without giving him a second look.

"Run," Walker begs. "Please, Tibby. Please go." He squeezes my hand, then drops it, shoving me away with what little strength he has. "You have to leave me. Now."

I'm barely listening to him. I push myself to my feet, staring at Lori in disbelief. "You killed him. You killed your husband. What kind of monster are you?"

She scoffs. "Come on, girlie. Try to keep up, will you? He's clearly not my husband. Did you really think I'd be married to someone like that? Please. Give me some credit. He's just some nobody I picked up and thought I could use for a while." She nods, swiping the knife in the snow with an evil grin. Everything about her has changed, like the flipping of a switch. No longer is she the sweet, innocent woman who called me terms of endearment, claimed to miss her daughter, and warned us to bundle up. Now, she's a monster. Empty yet filled with darkness. Everything from the way she walks to the tone of her voice has changed. "Kind of like you were for lover boy over there. And, hm, guess who's next?" She taps her finger on her chin, then her eyes widen with a wicked smile. "I'll bet you know."

"Just like you killed those kids?" I go on, testing a theory I'm nearly sure is right. "The couple whose car you're driving?"

She smiles. A confirmation if I've ever seen one.

"And Ernest?"

A wrinkle of confusion forms on her forehead. "Ernest? The manager?"

I nod.

The wrinkle disappears. "Ah, yes. Well, he saw his grandson's car being driven by someone who was not his grandson." She shrugs. "He asked too many questions. Left me no choice. He should've been more like that wife of his. Quiet. He would've been fine, then. He was in our room fixing the television when he saw the car, and he wouldn't let it go. I followed him to the lobby to shut him up while Tony took a shower."

I suck in a shallow breath. "The car... The boy that went missing, the boy whose car you have...was his grandson?" The bitter reality sets in. Someone out there will soon learn they've lost their son and father in one day.

She clicks her tongue, twirling the knife around haphazardly. "He didn't have to die. And, quite frankly, neither did either of you."

"Why did you kill the kids?" I take slow steps backward, maintaining the distance between us as she moves in my direction.

She shrugs one shoulder. "I needed a car."

"Why?" I can't breathe. Can't think. My mind feels like it's turned to ice right along with the snow beneath my feet.

She sneers, shaking her head. "You're asking too many questions, just like Ernest. Just like Tony. You saw what that got them."

I take another step back, my feet shuffling in the snow. She's right there with me. For every step I take, she takes two. Soon, she'll have caught up, and I'll be here, defenseless and weak for the second time in one night. The difference being that while Craig would only yell and threaten, Lori will actually kill me.

"There was only supposed to be one person dead tonight. A worthless cheater. He thought I was weak. All my life, people have underestimated me, and all my life, I've proven them wrong. Time after time, person after person. I'm sorry, Tabby." She says my name wrong with a sneer that tells me it was clearly on purpose. "You weren't supposed to be here. You or your boyfriend. But this is the path you chose."

"What are you talking about? We didn't choose anything! You slashed our tires and left us no choice.

You're the reason we're here. You had to have planned it all. You knew we'd need to leave and have no way to go anywhere without you."

She shakes her head. "Oh, you sweet, dumb girl. I didn't slash your tires."

"What are you talking about? Of course you did."

Her brows draw together. "Really? I've told you everything else I've done. Why would I lie about something as stupid as that? I didn't slash your tires. I had no reason to want you to travel with us. In fact, it was better for me if you stayed there at the motel. With the dead man in your room, no one would've been looking for me."

I let her words wash over me. "But...if you didn't do it..."

She waves the knife in Walker's direction, answering the question I can't bring myself to ask. "Narrow down your options, girlie. I managed to figure out this puzzle ages ago."

"Walker? He wouldn't."

She smirks, but doesn't argue.

"No. Why would he?" I glance over and find him staring at me from where he remains on the ground.

He blinks slowly.

"You didn't..."

"Tibby—"

"Please tell me you didn't." My voice cracks and I hate it. I hate myself for ever trusting him. For still wanting to trust him now.

"We heard you two fighting about how you wanted to leave," Lori says, drawing my attention back to her. "And shortly after, while I was taking care of Ernest, he went on his little walk." She chuckles to herself, tapping the knife to her temple. "Think. Use that pretty head for something other than growing hair. How else would I have known he had a knife, hmm? Why else would I have had Tony check him?"

I look down at Walker. Can it possibly be true? From where he lies, he lifts his head just slightly.

Tears blur my vision. "No lies, remember? We had a deal."

I can't bring myself to outright make the accusation, not when he's dying, but he makes the confession anyway. I deflate as the words leave his mouth. "I was... It was only about keeping...you...safe."

Because I'd wanted to leave, I realize. He didn't think it was safe, and he knew I'd never let it go. "You could've just hidden the keys," I point out, still in utter disbelief.

He tries to adjust in the snow, easing himself up slightly with his hands only to collapse again. "Yeah, but...there were only...so many places to hide them. You're...stubborn."

I shake my head. "That's completely insane. You realize that, right? Slashing your tires meant we'd be stuck there even after the storm cleared up."

One corner of his mouth upturns. "It wouldn't have been the worst thing."

"I didn't expect you to want to come with us," Lori

reiterates. "I planned to leave you there to deal with everything. Actually, I *wanted* to bury Ernest so there'd be nothing to deal with at all, but I had no shovel and the ground was frozen, and with the empty, unlocked room, it was just easier to drop him in your bathtub and disappear into the night. Less time away from Tony. Less time for him to be suspicious."

Suddenly, a memory flashes through my mind. I remember seeing a white car similar to the one Lori stole zipping past us after we left the rest area. I recall Walker's words.

You could've gotten a ride with them instead.

It could've been them who picked me up. Lori and Tony. I might've never met Walker. Never cared for him.

Because I do. I do care about him so much, and I want to tell him. I realize it now, but it's too late.

"Why would you let us come with you, then? Why not leave us there?"

"Because you'd seen me. It was too much of a risk to walk away and chance you telling the police what we looked like or what we were driving."

I take a step back again, horror filling my gut over how just a few wrong choices led us here, and Lori lunges at me.

"I don't have time for games," she shouts. "I have a plane to catch." She lunges again without warning, this time swiping my arm with her knife.

White-hot pain shoots through the limb. I cry out, folding in half and grabbing my arm. It happens fast, without much of a fight, even. Maybe I'm too tired, too weak. Maybe I'm still in shock. I'm not sure what it is, but try as I might, my body refuses to cooperate as I attempt to fight.

She shoves me down, and I fall. I try to stand, but she's faster. She brings the knife down into my stomach, and my body buckles in on itself. I cry out, screaming in agony as the searing pain shoots through me. It's like nothing I've ever felt before. A lightning bolt of pain traveling to every inch of my body. Like I'm being bathed in fire. As if my stomach is being ripped out of me. I cry and beg her to stop, wishing I'd stayed in the car with Craig. Wishing this entire night hadn't happened. Wishing I was somewhere safe and warm.

But then, I wouldn't have met Walker. Can I really wish that?

She lifts the knife and stabs me again. With the final blow, she sits back, swiping the back of her arm across her mouth. My blood is splattered across her face. My mind goes sharp with pain, yet fuzzy at the same time. My eyes travel across the snow to find him. It's the only thing that makes sense.

Throughout all of this, he's the only thing that makes me feel safe. Despite what he did, despite his lie, he's the only thing that will bring me comfort in my final moments.

I don't know where I am, where he is.

I need to find him.

My thoughts come back to me in bright-white focus. All of the fuzziness disappears at once.

He's not where he was.

Not anywhere.

I look left, right. *Where is he? Where am I?*

I'm fading again. Perhaps imagining all of this. If I close my eyes, I can pretend I'm still in bed. That this has all been some sort of dream. That I'm safe and warm and happy.

Then I hear Lori cry out, and my eyes tear open again.

"Walker?" As my eyes find focus, I see him. I realize he's on her back, squeezing her throat from behind. They fall into the snow together, and seconds later, I hear him groan as she stabs him again.

His screams tear through the night, bleeding into my brain, calling me to him. I don't know if any of this is real, but I hope some of it is. *Was.*

As I fade away, as I sink into nothingness, my last thought is of how badly I hope he was real.

Then it all goes black.

CHAPTER TWENTY-TWO

TIBBY

When my eyes open, everything is bright and ice cold. I didn't know I could see temperature, but at this moment, I swear I do. The cold seeps into my skin, my pores. I feel it in my eyes, my ears, my fingernails, my breath. It's everywhere, surrounding me. Swallowing me up.

At the same time, I'm completely numb. My body tingles and radiates and burns with that pins-and-needles feeling your feet get when they fall asleep.

Red-and-blue flashing lights splash over my face, reflecting on the snow all around me. I try to move my feet, my hands, to lift my head, but I can't. All I can do is lie completely still and pray for sleep again. Somewhere in the distance, I hear voices.

"And you don't know which way he went?" a man asks. It's a voice I don't recognize.

"That way, I think," the woman says. Her voice is

familiar. It sends a pang of anger through me. *Lori. Her name is Lori.* It comes back to me slowly. Who she is. What she's done. "He...he stabbed my friends, and I hid." She sobs. "I hid. I just did nothing...just hid and let them... I'm so sorry. I-I didn't know what else to do."

"And this same man, you'd seen him earlier in the night?" The man is no-nonsense, asking questions like he's reading off a script.

Someone is touching my arms, covering me with something. I can't open my eyes, but I swear they were open just moments ago. I can still see the flashing red-and-blue lights behind my eyelids, their rhythmic pattern almost hypnotizing.

"Yes. My husband and I stopped to help two teenagers that we thought were broken down. The man came out of nowhere. He stabbed my husband. He stabbed the kids. I...I just panicked. I ran. I took their car because our keys were in my husband's pocket, and I couldn't get to him. I couldn't... If I tried to get to him, I thought the man would get me. I just left him." She's talking through her sobs, practically in hysterics. "I stopped at the first place I could find because I couldn't get service, but the motel's phone lines were down, too. I was so scared. I didn't know what to do. I found some other guests, told them what had happened, and we tried to get help. They tried to help me. I was so distraught, so upset. I kept having panic attacks, and I couldn't even drive. I just want my husband back. I just want him back."

"Ma'am, I need you to breathe for me, okay? Tell me what happened next."

I hear her heavy, erratic breathing. "We drove to town together and called the police because the manager was dead, and they were supposed to come here. We saw flashing lights behind us and stopped, but it was...it was him. He found us again, just like he found me at the motel. It was so fast. He just killed them. There was nothing I could do."

"And how did you get blood all over you if you were hidden?" the officer asks.

"After he left, I...I didn't know what else to do. When I saw what he'd done, I tried to help. I did CPR. I tried to keep them warm, but they're all...they're all gone. My friends..."

"Your friends you met at the motel?"

"*Yes.*" She's crying again.

Something cold touches my chest, and I realize it's a hand. Someone is touching me. I will my eyes to open with every ounce of strength I have left.

"Okay. We just need you to calm down, ma'am. Everything's going to be alright. You're safe now. You're safe."

"I'm trying. It's so hard."

"I understand. You're just lucky the family drove by when they did. Good folks. Drove down all the way from Chicago to find their boy after they reported him missing earlier tonight. We're all lucky they just happened to see his car parked here. They almost missed ya. The dad's an officer up there in the city, so he knew just what to do. We'll let you talk to them at some point if you'd like, but for now, all you have to do is breathe. You're safe."

She's safe...and she's a liar, and she's going to get away with every bit of it. If the police hadn't arrived before she could leave, I'm sure she would be long gone by now.

"Wait a second." There's a woman's voice speaking near me. "He's breathing. We have a pulse."

He.

He who? Which *he*? I open my eyes then, finding the will deep within myself. I have to know if it's Walker. When I open my eyes, the hand on my chest pulls back, and a woman is staring down at me. She smiles broadly, and I turn my head, realizing Walker is lying next to me. He smiles, stretching his hand out slowly toward me, and I find the strength to smile back.

"Oh my god. They're both alive. Both of them," the woman announces, and suddenly more hands are on me. There are voices all around me, and I'm being poked and prodded and warmed.

Saved.

I'm being saved.

I look up to where Lori is standing, and even though I can't see her face clearly, I know she's looking at me. I can feel her horrified, furious stare burning holes into me, and I know exactly how she must feel.

The world goes dark and I realize I've closed my eyes

without meaning to. I'm beginning to drift off when I feel Walker's hand on my chest, bringing me back.

I open my eyes again, trying to find focus, and when I zero in on Lori once more, I feel a grin spread to my lips. Despite the pain still coursing through me, the grin on my lips is a cocky one. It's the kind of grin that says this night isn't going to go the way she thought it would after all.

She thought she'd won. She thought she had her story and plan all laid out. She was convincing, almost convincing enough, but there was one thing she didn't count on. One thing that will be her downfall. She has no idea how stubborn I am. It's always been my superpower. And right now, I'm just stubborn enough to survive. Turns out Walker is, too.

As if he can read my mind, Walker slowly slides his hand down my side and takes my hand in his. I glance over at him, and he smiles with his eyes closed. Weakly, he whispers, "Stubborn...ass."

I squeeze his hand gently just before I watch them lift and place him carefully onto a stretcher.

"You're going to be okay," the woman sitting next to me whispers, brushing the hair back from my face as I feel them begin to lift me next.

Yes, I think, looking only at Lori. It's a promise. A vow. She underestimated just how stubborn I can be. *Yes, I'm going to be just fine.*

WOULD YOU RECOMMEND THE STRANGER?

If you enjoyed this story, please consider leaving me a quick review. It doesn't have to be long—just a few words will do. Who knows? Your review might be the thing that encourages a future reader to take a chance on my work!

To leave a review, please visit:

kierstenmodglinauthor.com/thestranger

Let everyone know how much you loved *The Stranger* on Goodreads:

bit.ly/thestrangerkmod

STAY UP TO DATE ON EVERYTHING KMOD!

Thank you so much for reading this story. I'd love to invite you to sign up for my mailing list and text alerts so we can be sure you don't miss my next release.

Sign up for my mailing list here:
kierstenmodglinauthor.com/nlsignup

Sign up for my text alerts here:
kierstenmodglinauthor.com/textalerts

ACKNOWLEDGMENTS

When I set out to write this story, one thing I thought quite a lot about was trust. What makes us decide to trust someone? At what point do you decide that you do trust someone?

I've never been someone who trusts easily. Some of my worst memories come from being let down by friends and people I'd put my trust in, and so, from a young age, I've learned to keep my circle small. For me, writing about Tibby was like ripping off a bandage and taking a look at wounds I think most of us have. The pain that comes from trusting the wrong person with our hearts, our secrets, our bodies, and our lives and having them let us down in one way or another.

Because of the circumstances, because of the storm and everything else going on in the story, the risks for Tibby were heightened, but I think that's how it feels sometimes to put your trust in someone for the first time, whether it's a stranger or an old friend. It feels like you are risking everything. And when you've been let down before, it's easy to feel like a fool for being willing to risk being hurt ever again.

So this story was about trust for me, but also about

vulnerability and how hard it can be to be vulnerable for some people (hi! It's me). As with all my stories, the characters in this one changed me in ways I didn't expect. They reminded me of why we're willing to put our trust in people, and why it's always, always worth the risk. I think, if you look closely at all of my stories, there's always a hint of that. **Trust, safety, love, hope.** I've spent my life writing about these things underneath all the rest of it and I have to think it's because those are the things that are most important in the whole world. Those are the things that are always worth fighting for. Those are the things that are always worth the risk.

I'm more like Tibby than Walker, more cautious than outgoing, but Walker was a part of me too. He is the part that always wanted more friends, the part that looks forward to social situations, and the part that always wanted to feel like I belonged. Tibby is the part of me that got hurt by my friends, got left out, got talked about or made fun of when it suited them, she's the one who showed up at parties just to feel awkward, out of place, and unwanted. Tibby is the little girl in me (and maybe a bit in you, too) who never truly felt like she belonged anywhere.

If you saw yourself in these characters, I hope you found pieces of them both in you. Trust doesn't come easy to some of us, but when it does come, when someone earns your trust and shows up for you time and time again, it's a relationship to cherish and so, in a way, I owe this book to the people who've done that for me.

So, to all the "strangers" who've become my friends, my family, and my whole world, I owe you a tremendous amount of thanks:

To the world's best husband and sweetest little girl—thank you for being here for me. Thank you for cheering me on, celebrating with me, and always being in my corner. No one in the world knows me better than the two of you and I'm so grateful to know you both too. I love you so so much.

To my incredible editor, Sarah West—thank you for seeing my stories at their worst and helping me to bring out their best. There's no one I trust with these characters and their worlds more than you.

To the awesome proofreading team at My Brother's Editor—thank you for being my final set of eyes on each story and never letting me down.

To my loyal readers (AKA the #KMod Squad)—thank you for everything you do for me. You guys are the reason I get to do this, you're the reason I'm living my dream, and you're the reason I've learned to trust myself and my instincts. When I first started this journey and no one was willing to take a risk on me, you guys did. You showed up and proved the ones who had doubted me wrong. And, here we are, eight years later, and you just keep showing up. You were my greatest wish and I can't put into words how much your support has meant to me and continues to mean to me. When I sit down at my computer every day, before I type a single word, I think of you. Thank you for trusting me to entertain you. There's not a higher compliment you could give me.

To my book club/gang/besties—Sara, both Erins, June, Heather, and Dee—thank you for showing me true friendship in its rawest and most beautiful form. I can't tell you ladies how much these past few years calling you my friends has meant to me. I'm so grateful for your consistency and kindness, for our laughs and adventures, and for the way you've shown up for me in the most amazing and unexpected ways possible. I love you guys so much.

To my bestie, Emerald O'Brien—thank you for being the one I trust with everything. From story ideas to family drama, you have been my rock throughout so much and I love, admire, and am so grateful for you.

To Becca and Lexy—thank you both for showing up when I needed you and continuing to stick around. I'm so thankful to have you in my corner.

To my agent, Carly, and my audiobook publishing team at Dreamscape—thank you for putting your trust in me and helping to get these books into the most hands possible.

Last but certainly not least, to you, dear reader—thank you for trusting me to tell this story. Thank you for seeing the cover or my name, for listening to your friend's recommendation, that social media post, or seeing this book out in the wild and deciding to take a chance on it. Your trust is something I will never take for granted. When I write these stories, I think of you. I wonder which parts will stick with you, which ones you'll enjoy, which moments will shock you, and which characters you'll love or hate. I truly hope you enjoyed Tibby's story. And, as always, whether this is your first Kiersten Modglin novel or your 43rd, my greatest wish is that it was everything you hoped for and nothing like you expected.

ABOUT THE AUTHOR

KIERSTEN MODGLIN is a Top 10 bestselling author of psychological thrillers. Her books have sold over a million copies and been translated into multiple languages. Kiersten is a member of International Thriller Writers, Novelists, Inc., and the Alliance of Independent Authors. She is a KDP Select All-Star and a recipient of *ThrillerFix*'s Best Psychological Thriller Award, *Suspense Magazine*'s Best Book of 2021 Award, a 2022 Silver Falchion for Best Suspense, and a 2022 Silver Falchion for Best Overall Book of 2021. Kiersten grew up in rural western Kentucky and later relocated to Nashville, Tennessee, where she now lives with her family. Kiersten's readers across the world lovingly refer to her as

"KMod." A binge-watching expert, psychology fanatic, and *indoor* enthusiast, Kiersten enjoys rainy days spent with her favorite people and evenings with her nose in a book.

Sign up for Kiersten's newsletter here:
kierstenmodglinauthor.com/nlsignup

Sign up for text alerts from Kiersten here:
kierstenmodglinauthor.com/textalerts

kierstenmodglinauthor.com
www.facebook.com/kierstenmodglinauthor
www.facebook.com/groups/kmodsquad
www.twitter.com/kmodglinauthor
www.instagram.com/kierstenmodglinauthor
www.tiktok.com/@kierstenmodglinauthor
www.goodreads.com/kierstenmodglinauthor
www.bookbub.com/authors/kiersten-modglin

ALSO BY KIERSTEN MODGLIN

STANDALONE NOVELS

Becoming Mrs. Abbott

The List

The Missing Piece

Playing Jenna

The Beginning After

The Better Choice

The Good Neighbors

The Lucky Ones

I Said Yes

The Mother-in-Law

The Dream Job

The Nanny's Secret

The Liar's Wife

My Husband's Secret

The Perfect Getaway

The Roommate

The Missing

Just Married

Our Little Secret

Widow Falls

Missing Daughter

The Reunion

Tell Me the Truth

The Dinner Guests

If You're Reading This...

A Quiet Retreat

The Family Secret

Don't Go Down There

Wait for Dark

You Can Trust Me

Hemlock

Do Not Open

You'll Never Know I'm Here

The Stranger

ARRANGEMENT TRILOGY

The Arrangement (Book 1)

The Amendment (Book 2)

The Atonement (Book 3)

THE MESSES SERIES

The Cleaner (Book 1)

The Healer (Book 2)

The Liar (Book 3)

The Prisoner (Book 4)

<u>NOVELLAS</u>

The Long Route: A Lover's Landing Novella

The Stranger in the Woods: A Crimson Falls Novella